James

THE PILLAR OF THE EARLY CHURCH

James
THE PILLAR OF THE EARLY CHURCH

Lucidus. S
28/5/17

Also by Lucidus Smith

Fiction
The 'Blossom' Trilogy

    Oh for a Ha'porth of Tar

    Blossom in Winter – Frost in Spring

    Blossom by the Billabong

The Red Rabbit Inquiry Agency –
Books One, Two, Three & Four

The Lost Treasure of Pim de Zwolle
    (A 17th Century Pirate)

The Buidhe Galaxy

The Team that Bowled at Hotham Springs

Non-Fiction
The Business of Waterways management
    (A toe in the water)

James
THE PILLAR OF THE EARLY CHURCH

A 21st Century Commentary

LUCIDUS SMITH

authorHOUSE

AuthorHouse™ UK
1663 Liberty Drive
Bloomington, IN 47403 USA
www.authorhouse.co.uk
Phone: 0800.197.4150

© 2017 Lucidus Smith. All rights reserved.

No part of this book may be reproduced, stored in a retrieval system, or transmitted by any means without the written permission of the author.

Scripture quotations are the author's paraphrase of the Holy Bible, King James Version (Authorized Version). First published in 1611. Quoted from the KJV Classic Reference Bible, Copyright © 1983 by The Zondervan Corporation.

Scripture quotations marked NIV are taken from the Holy Bible, New International Version®. NIV®. Copyright © 1973, 1978, 1984 by International Bible Society. Used by permission of Zondervan. All rights reserved. [Biblica]

Published by AuthorHouse 04/03/2017

ISBN: 978-1-5246-7924-8 (sc)
ISBN: 978-1-5246-7923-1 (e)

Print information available on the last page.

Any people depicted in stock imagery provided by Thinkstock are models, and such images are being used for illustrative purposes only. Certain stock imagery © Thinkstock.

This book is printed on acid-free paper.

Because of the dynamic nature of the Internet, any web addresses or links contained in this book may have changed since publication and may no longer be valid. The views expressed in this work are solely those of the author and do not necessarily reflect the views of the publisher, and the publisher hereby disclaims any responsibility for them.

DEDICATION

To the saintly men and women of Northcote Road Baptist Church in Battersea, South London who during the 1940's, 50's and 60's taught me and mentored me in the things of Christ and in particular to Mr. H. Matson and Mr. Jerry Davis.

Foreword

Those of us who are Christians, followers of Jesus Christ, have embarked on a journey of life, intent on doing our best to exhibit the character and qualities of Jesus so that others also may come to know, love and follow Him too!

Each one of us who has come to know Christ has a story to share. It's an individual story of how the Lord has led and guided us along the way, a story of what He has done in our lives.

I have come to know and appreciate the author of this book over several years. As I read it I read his story as it is based on the Biblical instruction and guidance of its author James.

God's Word has been placed in our hands as a life guide and an instruction manual as to how we are to live and be as God's committed and devoted followers.

The author of this work has taken a combination of the instructive words of James and his own life experience of those instructions to provide us with an example of how we too may live a life worthy of Jesus Christ our Lord. Lucidus does not pretend to be perfect, and in fact in places shares with us some of his failings, however, always the lessons learnt have enabled him to grow from strength to strength in his quest to be a devoted disciple of Jesus.

This book gives us a real insight as to how 'ordinary' Christians may live as God's people, and I believe, offers the reader true encouragement as to how to apply God's good principles for life to all those desirous of pleasing God.

The authors intent, I believe, is to offer the reader a sort of 'how to' in the hope that it will result in that person becoming more aware of how much the Lord God knows them and loves them and how much He wants the best for their lives.

I commend this Book, 'James, The Pillar of the Early Church,' a 21st Century Commentary by Lucidus Smith to you. I believe it will be a good help to you in your Christian journey.

Allan Harrison
Chaplain – Silver Chain Hospice Care – Mandurah WA

Table of Contents

Introduction xi

Chapter 1	The New Testament Book of James.............	1
Chapter 2	Other Bible References for James................	16
Chapter 3	Commentary - James - Chapter One	19
Chapter 4	Commentary - James - Chapter Two	50
Chapter 5	Commentary - James - Chapter Three	80
Chapter 6	Commentary - James - Chapter Four.......	101
Chapter 7	Commentary - James - Chapter Five.......	126
Chapter 8	Synopsis of the Book of James.................	155
Chapter 9	Prayers you may find useful	159
Chapter 10	A Short Study on the Ten Commandments......................................	172

Introduction

The New Testament book of James, the Lord Jesus' brother, has always been one of my favourite books in the whole bible, as in my opinion it gives a clear picture of how we should function as individual Christian believers and how believers and the local church or fellowship that they are part of, should interact together.

During the summer of 2016 I felt prompted to write my own paraphrase of the Book of James, based on the King James Version of the bible and then in early December, after a conversation with a friend of mine at church, I felt the time was right to write my own Commentary on James with language and examples from the modern era.

All bible references in this book are once again my own paraphrase, based on the King James Version of the bible.

I hope you find this book challenging, stimulating and helpful in your Christian walk and that it encourages you to get to know the bible more deeply in the future.

Lucidus Smith

Chapter One

THE NEW TESTAMENT BOOK OF JAMES

(BELIEVED TO BE THE BROTHER OF JESUS)

The King James Version of the bible as revised and paraphrased by Lucidus Smith

Chapter One

1. James, a slave (or servant) of God and of the Lord Jesus Christ, greetings to the twelve tribes in the dispersion (or those believers not found in Jerusalem).

2. My brothers, count it as something joyful when you fall into different sorts of trials;

3. Knowing that when your faith is tested in this way and that you are able to overcome the trial, then this experience will build endurance within you.

4. And let this endurance work in you in order that you may be made perfect and complete, wanting in nothing.

5. But if any one of you wants wisdom, let him ask God for it and it will be given to him; for he is the one who gives wisdom to all men, without reservation and without reproach.

6. But let him ask in faith, without doubting that he will receive what he has asked for, for the one who doubts is like a wave of the sea which is driven by the wind and is tossed about.

7. For that man should not suppose that he will receive anything from the Lord,

8. Because someone who is two minded about things is unsettled in all that he does.

9. But let the humble brother boast in his high position;

10. And let the rich brother boast of his humble position, because just like a flower of the grass, he will pass away.

11. For as soon as the sun rose in the sky it produced a hot wind which dried the grass and the flower withered and fell apart and its beauty perished; so also the rich man, while he is going here and there, will fade away.

12. Blessed is the man who remains faithful throughout a trial, because having become approved (by God), he

will receive the crown of life which he promised to those who love him.

13. Let no man say when he is being tempted that the temptation comes from God, for God cannot be tempted with evil and neither does he tempt anyone.

14. But each man is tempted when he is drawn away from God by the lusts of his own heart which he finds enticing;

15. So lust then, having been conceived gives birth to sin and sin, having been fully formed, brings about death.

16. Do not go astray (be deceived), my beloved brothers.

17. Every act of good giving and every perfect gift comes down from above, from the Father of lights, with whom there is neither variation nor shadow of turning.

18. Having resolved (what to do), he brought us forth by the word of truth, that we should be a kind of first-fruits of his creatures.

19. Understand this, my beloved brothers, let every man be swift to hear, slow to speak and slow to get angry;

20. For the anger of a man does not work the righteousness of God (does not cause the righteousness of God to function).

21. Therefore, putting away all filthiness and the unnecessary abundance of evil, receive with meekness the implanted word, which is able to save your souls.

22. And (what is more), become doers of the word and not just hearers, otherwise you would be misleading yourselves.

23. Because if anyone is a hearer of the word and not a doer, he is like a man who looks at his own face in a mirror,

24. And having looked at himself, goes away and immediately forgets what he looked like.

25. But the person who having looked into the perfect law of freedom (which sets us free) and continues in doing this, not being a forgetful hearer, but a doer of the work (of what it says), this person shall be blessed in what he undertakes.

26. If anyone thinks of himself as being religious and does not have control of his own tongue then he is just deceiving himself and his religion is futile and fruitless.

27. Religion which God the Father considers to be clean and undefiled is this, to visit orphans and widows when they are distressed and to keep oneself unspotted (untainted and uncontaminated) from the world.

Chapter Two

1. My brothers, having faith in our glorious Lord Jesus Christ you must treat everyone equally (and not show more respect to one person than another).

2. For if a well dressed man should come into your meeting with a gold ring on his finger along with a poor man in shabby clothing,

3. And you look at the man wearing the expensive clothes and say, 'here's a nice seat, why don't you sit down here' and to the poor man say, 'you can stand over there or sit here on the floor by me':

4. Have you not shown discrimination among yourselves and become guilty of making judgements based on evil thoughts (wrong standards).

5. Listen to me, my beloved brothers; has not God chosen the poor of this world to be rich in faith and heirs of the kingdom which he promised those that love him?

6. But you dishonour the poor man. Is it not the rich men who oppress you and drag you into court?

7. Do they not blaspheme the good name by which you have been called?

8. If indeed you are fulfilling the royal law according to scripture, 'you shall love your neighbour as yourself;' you are doing well:

9. But if you are showing discrimination with regard to people, you are committing a sin and will be convicted by the law as transgressors (lawbreakers).

10. For he who keeps the whole law, yet stumbles in just one thing, has become guilty of breaking all of it.

11. For the one who said, 'Do not commit adultery', also said, 'Do not murder', now if you do not commit adultery but you do murder, you have become a transgressor of the law (a lawbreaker).

12. So, you should speak and behave as though you were about to be judged by a law of freedom:

13. For judgement will be without mercy for the person who has not shown mercy; mercy exults (is joyfully triumphant) over judgement.

14. What profit is there my brothers, if anyone says that they have faith but does not have works (actions to demonstrate that faith)? Do you think that faith like that can save him?

15. If a brother or sister is naked, or is lacking enough food for each day,

16. And one of you says to them, 'Go in peace, be warm (well clothed) and well fed'; but does not give them anything to meet their bodily needs, what is the good of that?

17. In the same way, faith on its own, without works, is dead.

18. But someone will say, 'you have faith and I have works, show me (demonstrate to me) your faith without your works and I will show you (demonstrate to you) my faith, by means of my works.'

19. Do you believe that there is one God? Good for you; the demons also believe that and shudder.

20. But are you willing to know (understand, accept), O vain man (you useless, fruitless, insignificant, empty person) that faith without works is barren (sterile, unproductive)?

21. Was not our father Abraham justified by works by offering up his son Isaac on the altar?

22. You can see that faith worked (in conjunction) with his works and by the works, the faith was made perfect;

23. And the scripture was fulfilled which said, 'And Abraham believed God and it was reckoned (counted, considered) to him as righteousness' and he was called the friend of God.

24. You see then that by works a man is justified and not by faith alone.

25. In the same way, was not Rahab the prostitute justified by works, when she entertained the messengers (the

spies sent out by Joshua) and sent them on their way by a different route?

26. For as the body without the spirit is dead, so also is faith dead without works.

Chapter Three

1. My brothers, (I advise that) not many of you should become teachers, because you know that we (who are teachers) will receive a greater judgement (will be judged more severely).

2. For in many respects we all stumble (we all make mistakes); but if someone does not stumble with regard to the things he says, then that person is a perfect man and is able to bridle (control) his whole body.

3. Behold, we put bits into the mouths of horses in order to make them obey us and (through those bits) we can direct their whole bodies.

4. Consider also ships, which though they are so great and are driven along by strong winds yet are steered by a very little helm (rudder) wherever the person steering it should decide to go.

5. Even so, the tongue is also a small member but is capable of being very boastful. Just think of how a small fire can burn down a great wood!

6. And the tongue is a fire, acting as a world of iniquity; as it sits among the members of our bodies, staining the whole body and inflaming the course of nature (setting the direction of a person's life on fire) and it is set on fire itself, by hell.

7. For every kind of beast, whether birds, or reptiles or marine creatures is tamed and has been tamed by man;

8. But no man is able to tame the tongue; it is an unruly evil, full of deadly poison.

9. By this tongue we bless the Lord and Father and by the same tongue we curse our fellow man who has been created in the likeness of God:

10. So that out of the same mouth comes forth both blessing and cursing. My brothers, these things ought not to be.

11. Can a fountain (or spring) send out both sweet and bitter water from the same hole?

12. My brothers, can a fig tree produce olives or a vine produce figs? Neither can a salt water fountain (or spring) make sweet water.

13. Who among you is wise and has understanding? Let him show it by his good conduct, by his works which are carried out in the humility which comes from wisdom.

14. But if you have bitter jealousy and rivalry in your hearts, do not be jubilant about it and lie against (deny) the truth.

15. This wisdom has not come down from above, but is earthly, sensual, of the devil.

16. For where jealousy and rivalry are, there is tumult (uproar, confusion, disturbance) and every evil practice.

17. But the wisdom which is from above is first of all pure, then peaceable (quiet, tranquil, peaceful, not at war), self-controlled, submissive, full of mercy and good fruits, without partiality and hypocrisy.

18. When peacemakers sow in peace there is a harvest of righteousness.

Chapter Four

1. From where do wars and fighting among you come? Do they not come as a result of the desires which are battling within you?

2. You desire and don't have (what you desire); you murder and are jealous and are not able to obtain (what you want); you fight and you war. You do not have because you do not ask.

3. When you ask, you do not receive, as you are asking for the wrong things; because you want them to indulge your own pleasures.

4. You adulterers and adulteresses, don't you know that friendship with the world is enmity (hostility, hatred, animosity) towards God? Whoever therefore, resolves to be a friend of the world is establishing themselves as an enemy of God.

5. Or do you think that the scripture says for no reason that 'The Spirit which dwells in you enviously desires (after worldly pleasures)'.

6. But the grace he gives us is even greater; for which reason scripture says, 'God resists those who are arrogant but he gives grace to those who are humble'.

7. Submit yourselves therefore, to God; but oppose the devil and he will flee from you.

8. Draw near to God and he will draw near to you. Cleanse your hands you sinners and purify your hearts you double minded (hypocrites).

9. Be distressed and mourn and weep; let your laughter be turned to mourning and your joy to dejection (heaviness, depression).

10. Humble yourselves before the Lord and he will exalt you (raise you up).

11. Do not speak against one another brothers. Whoever speaks against his brother or judges his brother speaks against the law and judges the law, and if you judge the law you are not a doer of the law but a judge (of the law).

12. There is one lawgiver and judge who is able to save and to destroy; so who are you to judge your neighbour?

13. Come now (and pay attention) all of you who say: Today or tomorrow we will go into this city and we will stay there for a year and trade and make a profit.

14. You do not know what will happen to you tomorrow. For you are a vapour (a mist), appearing for a little while and then you have completely disappeared (vanished).

15. Instead you should be saying: If it is the Lord's will we will be alive and we will be doing this and that.

16. But as it is you brag about your boastful language; all such boastings are evil.

17. Therefore (I say) to the person who knows the good he ought to do and fails to do it, such a failure is a sin.

Chapter Five

1. Come now (and pay attention) you rich people, weep and cry aloud over the hardships which are coming upon you.

2. Your riches have become corrupted and your garments have become moth-eaten.

3. Your gold and silver have become rusted over (corrupted) and the poison resulting from this corruption will be a testimony against you and it will consume your flesh like fire. You have stored up treasure in these last days.

4. Behold, the wages of the workmen who have reaped your lands which you have kept back (and not paid to them), cry out and the cries of those who have been reaping have entered the ears of (been heard by) the Lord of Hosts.

5. You have lived in luxury on the earth and have lived riotously (without restraint, running wild) you nourished your own hearts as in a day of slaughter.

6. You have condemned and murdered innocent people; even though they were not resisting you.

7. Therefore, be longsuffering (patient, enduring insult) brothers, until the coming of the Lord. Behold (consider) the farmer as he waits for the precious crop which the earth produces, watching patiently over it until he gets both the early and late rains.

8. You also must be longsuffering, settle your hearts, because the coming of the Lord is near.

9. Do not murmur against (complain about, disparage) one another brothers, for fear that you will be judged; for behold, the judge is standing at the door.

10. As an example of longsuffering under persecution my brothers, take the prophets who spoke in the name of the Lord.

11. Behold, we consider those who have endured, to be blessed. You have heard of the endurance of Job and you know of the final outcome that he received from the Lord, for the Lord is compassionate and merciful.

12. But above everything else my brothers, do not swear; neither by heaven nor by earth, nor by any other oath; but let your 'Yes' be 'yes' and your 'No' be 'no', so that you do not fall under judgement.

13. Is anyone among you in trouble (afflicted)? Let him pray. Is anyone cheerful (or merry)? Let him sing a psalm.

14. Is anyone among you sick? Let him summon the elders of the church and let them pray over him, having anointed him with oil in the name of the Lord.

15. And the prayer of faith will heal the one who is sick and the Lord will raise him and if he has sinned it will be forgiven him.

16. Therefore, confess your sins to one another and pray on behalf of one another so that you might be healed. The fervent prayer of a righteous man is extremely effective.

17. Elijah was a man with feelings, just like us and he prayed earnestly that it would not rain and it did not rain on the earth for three years and six months.

18. And he prayed again and the heavens gave rain and the earth brought forth all of its fruits.

19. My brothers, if anyone among you wanders from the truth and another one of you turns him back to the truth again;

20. You should know this, that the person who turns a sinner from the error of his way will save his soul from death and will hide a multitude of sins.

THE END

Chapter Two

OTHER BIBLE REFERENCES FOR JAMES

Matthew Chapter 13 Verse 55
(Also Mark Chapter 6 Verse 3)
We are told that after Jesus spoke in the synagogue in his home town of Nazareth that someone present made the comment, 'Isn't this the son of the carpenter? Isn't his mother named Mary and his brothers are James, Joses, Simon and Judas (Jude)?

Acts Chapter 12 Verse 17
After Peter escaped from prison he went to the house of Mary the mother of John, where a group of believers had met together and were praying and he told them to let James and the other brothers know that he was now free.

We already know from Acts Chapter 12 Verse 2 that Herod had executed James the brother of John so this James that Peter referred to was indeed the Lord's brother.

Acts Chapter 15 Verse 13

Verse 6 tells us that the elders and apostles had come together to discuss the matter of circumcision and verse 12 tells us that Barnabas and Paul addressed the meeting and after they had finished speaking that James answered in support of what Barnabas and Paul had been saying, thus showing that he was a man of importance and a member of this elite group.

Acts Chapter 21 Verse 18

Again James is mentioned as being present along with the elders.

1 Corinthians Chapter 15 Verse 7

Paul testifies that the Lord was seen after he had risen from the dead by James and then by all of the apostles.

Galatians Chapter 1 Verses 18 & 19

Paul tells us that after a period of three years he went up to Jerusalem but the only person he saw apart from Peter was the Lord's brother James.

Galatians Chapter 2 Verses 9

On another trip to Jerusalem (verse 2 says that it was after fourteen years) Paul makes the comment that James, Cephas (Peter) and John seemed to be 'Pillars' of the church.

Galatians Chapter 2 Verses 12

In this verse James is accredited by Paul with sending men to Antioch, this being another indication of his importance and seniority in the early church.

Book of Jude Verse 1

In his greeting to the recipients of his letter Jude refers to himself as a servant of Jesus Christ and a brother of James (see Matthew Chapter 13 Verse 55).

Chapter Three

COMMENTARY ON THE BOOK OF JAMES

Chapter One

1. James, a slave (or servant) of God and of the Lord Jesus Christ, greetings to the twelve tribes in the dispersion (or those believers not found in Jerusalem).

What a humble man James must have been, to refer to himself as a slave or servant of God. He doesn't call himself 'Archbishop James' or 'The Very Reverend James' or 'Senior Pastor James' and not even 'Father James' but simply James; nor does he make mention of the fact that he was the Lord's brother but is happy to call himself God's slave or servant.

Are you concerned about being addressed by the correct title and letting people know what an important person you are in the church?

Do you think of yourself as a servant?

Remember what Jesus said in Matthew Chapter 20 Verse 27:

Whoever would be chief (first) among you, let him be your slave (servant).

Apart from his humility James was showing concern for those who were not living in Jerusalem but were spread throughout the rest of the known world; this letter was for them. He was saying, "We haven't forgotten about you and you are important to us."

There is a danger in these days of 'Social Media' to take the view that everyone can find out what is going on at the centre of things, if they choose to and that might well be correct, up to a point, but it doesn't stop them from feeling left out and ignored and marginalised.

There is nothing like personal contact, be it a visit, a letter or a telephone call, to make people feel that they belong and are not just there to pay the bills or do the work.

2. My brothers, count it as something joyful when you fall into different sorts of trials;

I have to admit that my reaction to this verse is, "I'm sorry, but can we take a vote on this one? I didn't join up to fall into different sorts of trials or troubles!"

But then I remember the incident recorded in the Gospel of Luke Chapter 13 verses 1 to 5 which I believe is an indication that we can all be affected by unpleasant accidents and situations:

And there were some people present, at that time, who told him about the Galileans whose blood Pilate had mixed with their sacrifices.

And answering, he said to them: Do you think that these Galileans are greater sinners than all other Galileans because they had to suffer these things?

No – I tell you, but unless you repent, you will all perish likewise.

Or those eighteen, upon whom the tower in Siloam fell and killed them: do you thing that they were greater sinners than everyone else living in Jerusalem?

No – I tell you, but unless you repent, you will similarly perish.

Added to which Jesus did say in Luke Chapter 9 Verse 23:

If anyone wishes to come after me, let him deny himself, and daily take up his cross and let him follow me.

So it would appear that apart from suffering the same sort of accidental trials that the rest of humanity have to face, as Christians, we may have to suffer other trials, because of our faith.

But, I hear you ask, why should that be so?
The answer is given by James in Verses 3 and 4.

3. Knowing that when your faith is tested in this way and that you are able to overcome the trial, then this experience will build endurance within you.

4. And let this endurance work in you in order that you may be made perfect and complete, wanting in nothing.

The apostle Paul confirmed James's view on overcoming trials when he wrote in 1 Corinthians Chapter 10 Verse 13:
You have not had any temptations, except those which are common to all men; but we have a faithful God, who will not allow you to be tempted beyond what you are able to bear; but will, with the temptation, make a way of escape for you, so that you are able to endure it.

The word 'endure' means to undergo difficulty, hardship, strain or privation without giving in or yielding to it and 'endurance' is the capacity to endure.

In Ephesians Chapter 6 Verses 10 to 20 Paul talks about putting on the 'Armour of God' the purpose of which is summed up in verse 13 where he explains:
Therefore take for yourselves, the whole armour of God, in order that you may be able to resist the evil which comes against you each day and after everything has happened to you, to stand.

The armour of God allows us to endure the trials and bad experiences that happen to us during our Christian lives so that we do not become like the seed which fell on rocky ground in the Parable of the Sower (Luke Chapter 8 Verses 1 to 15) where we are told in verse 13:
And the ones on the rocky ground are those that hear the word and receive it with joy, but do not develop proper

roots, so they believe for a while, but fall away in difficult times.

Instead, we want to be numbered among the seed that fell onto good ground as described in Verse 15:
But the ones in the good soil, well these are the ones with a good and honest heart, on hearing the word they hold on to it (nothing takes it from them), and patiently produce a harvest.

James Chapter 1 Verse 4 talks about being 'made perfect and complete, wanting in nothing.'
Paul confirms this in Colossians Chapter 2 Verse 10 where he says:
And you are complete in him, who is the head of all rule and authority.

You are complete and made perfect in Christ, don't let the devil or anyone else ever tell you otherwise.

5. But if any one of you wants wisdom, let him ask God for it and it will be given to him; for he is the one who gives wisdom to all men, without reservation and without reproach.

When was the last time you asked for wisdom?
There are no conditions attached to asking God for wisdom. Whether you are at work, at home, at church, at play, out shopping, fishing or anywhere else for that matter, wisdom is always a great thing to be equipped with.

How often do we launch off into prayer for someone or something, without asking God to give us wisdom about how we should pray?

I recall being in a prayer meeting many years ago when we felt led to pray for three different sick people, all of whom had similar symptoms. The leader of the meeting asked for wisdom as to how we should pray for these three people and the answer we got back was completely different for each one of them.

The Book of Proverbs is primarily about wisdom and King Solomon's view of those not having it is clearly stated in Chapter 1 Verse 7:

The fear of the Lord is the beginning of knowledge, but fools despise wisdom and instruction.

Today the word 'fool' does not have a great impact on us but remember the parable of the two men who built houses in Matthew Chapter 7 Verses 24 to 27 and the one who built his house upon the sand which was destroyed by the rain and floods (Verse 26) was described as 'foolish' by Jesus!

At the start of every day make a point of asking God to give you wisdom for every situation you may find yourself in that day.

6. But let him ask in faith, without doubting that he will receive what he has asked for, for the one who doubts is like a wave of the sea which is driven by the wind and is tossed about.

In Luke Chapter 17 Verse 6 Jesus said:

If you have faith the size of a mustard seed, you would have said to this sycamore tree: Be uprooted and be planted in the sea. And it would have obeyed you.

And again in Matthew Chapter 17 Verse 20 he said:
For truly I say to you, that if you had faith the size of a mustard seed, you would say to this mountain: Move away from here; and it would be removed and nothing would be impossible to you.

I have often thought about casting things into the sea but I know my faith is not that great. I remember driving past Ben Nevis once on a trip to Scotland and considered having that cast into the sea, but then I thought of the massive splash it would make and the people who might be walking on it at the time and decided against it.

How hard it is to pray for something that you don't truly have the faith to believe can happen.
For me the secret is to pray for what I do believe can happen.
My wife and I were visiting a lady from our church whose husband was severely ill with back pain. He was only a young man but when we went round to see them he was lying down flat on the living room floor and could not move.
Prompted by the Holy Spirit I told him that we would be happy to pray for him but felt I needed to be honest with him, as he was not a Christian at that time and told him that the limit of my faith was to believe that he would be much improved by the time that six months had gone by.

He replied that six months was acceptable and allowed us to pray for him. By the time that six months had passed he was up off the floor and leading an active life once again.

As a result of praying for this man's back my wife and I had a boost of faith which has allowed us to pray for lots of other people's backs since then, virtually all of which have received a measure of healing, be it quickly or gradually, miraculously or through the ministration of doctors and nurses.

And remember, like the father of the boy who was healed after Jesus came down from the Mount of Transfiguration in Mark Chapter 9 Verse 24, we too can say:

Lord, I believe, help me to overcome my unbelief.

7. For that man should not suppose that he will receive anything from the Lord,

8. Because someone who is two minded about things is unsettled in all that he does.

Would you want to give the keys of your brand new car to someone you didn't know very well, or to someone who hadn't driven for twenty years, or wasn't certain how to operate the controls, or which side of the road to drive on?

Of course you wouldn't, as they could well be a danger to themselves and to other road users, apart from the damage they might do to your new car or to your good name if they acted illegally or unconscionably.

It is not surprising, therefore, to discover in Verse 8 that the Lord is also 'picky' about who he gives his gifts to and in particular he is likely to ignore the requests of someone who is two minded or unsettled.

In Luke Chapter 9 Verses 61 the writer records an incident when someone came to Jesus and said:
I will follow you, Lord; but first allow me to say farewell to the people in my house.
Jesus' reply was very blunt and sums up the issue of being two minded, he said:
No man, having put his hand to the plough and looking at the things left behind, is fit for the kingdom of God.

If we put Jesus first in our lives we will not be 'two minded' but 'single minded' as we seek to serve him and ask him to equip us for the task.

9. But let the humble brother boast in his high position;

10. And let the rich brother boast of his humble position, because just like a flower of the grass, he will pass away.

11. For as soon as the sun rose in the sky it produced a hot wind which dried the grass and the flower withered and fell apart and its beauty perished; so also the rich man, while he is going here and there, will fade away.

I wonder if James had the Sermon on the Mount in mind (Luke Chapter 6 Verses 20 to 26) when he wrote Verses 9 to 11.

And he (Jesus), looking at his disciples said:

Blessed are the poor, because yours is the kingdom of God.

Blessed are the ones who are hungry now, because you will be satisfied: Blessed are the ones who are weeping now, because you will laugh.

Blessed are you when men hate you and ostracise you and pick on you and speak your name as if it is something evil, for the Son of man's sake.

When that day happens, rejoice and leap for joy, (for I tell you,) that your reward in heaven is great: for their fathers did exactly the same things to the prophets.

But watch out, you who are rich, for you have already received your reward.

Watch out, you who have been filled now, for you will be hungry; watch out, you who are laughing now, for you will be sad and will cry.

Watch out, when men speak well of you: for their fathers did exactly the same to the false prophets.

Proverbs Chapter 16 Verse 19 warns us:

It is better to be of a humble spirit with the lowly than to divide the spoil with the proud.

How many of yesterday's 'front page' celebrities do not even make page six today?

How many leading politicians, businessmen and TV icons of just a few years ago are 'has beens' today?

I love 'Day Lilies' and bright yellow 'Cannas' and have had both flowers in my gardens over the years, but those blooms last but a day and then they are gone whereas other flowers like 'Tulips' and 'Daffodils' can last for several weeks.

A meteoric rise to fame and fortune is often followed by a meteoric fall, so be wary of what you wish for and do not be envious of those who have the things of this world which will pass away but seek to store up for yourself treasure in heaven which will last for eternity.

12A. Blessed is the man who remains faithful throughout a trial,

A few years ago a young friend of mine telephoned me in a very distressed frame of mind. People close to him had been blackening his name and he did not know what to do about it, as everyone seemed to be against him.

He and I had not spoken for more than ten years but I persuaded him to tell me what people were saying about him and without hesitation I told him that I did not believe a word of it.

He started to get emotional and thanked me for having faith in him and said that he now felt he had the confidence to fight these people and clear his name.

We all need good, reliable friends in times of trouble and so does our Lord Jesus. Being let down or betrayed or maligned by someone we thought was our true friend is one of the most painful experiences anyone can ever go through, it equates to grief in the debilitating effect it can have on you.

I believe Jesus feels the same level of hurt every time we, his followers let him down. A prayer I sometimes use when I think I am in for a difficult day goes as follows:

Lord Jesus, please keep me from situations today where I would let you down, but if I do happen to find myself in such a situation, please strengthen me so that I can stay faithful to you. Amen.

I am sure we all want to hear those special words when we meet our Lord face to face, recorded by Matthew in Chapter 25 Verse 21 in the parable of the talents:

Well done, my good and faithful servant, enter into the joy of your Lord.

12B. because having become approved (by God), he will receive the crown of life which he promised to those who love him.

In Proverbs Chapter 4 Verse 9 we are told:
She (wisdom) will deliver to you a 'crown of glory'.

1 Peter Chapter 5 Verse 4 tells us:
When the Chief Shepherd (Jesus) appears, you shall receive a crown of glory that does not fade.

Revelation Chapter 2 Verse 10 confirms:
Do not be fearful about any of these things which you are about to suffer;
But, be faithful unto death and I will give you the crown of life.

Just think, a crown is the sign of kingship and that is how important we are to Jesus and how much he values our faithfulness and our love.

13. Let no man say when he is being tempted that the temptation comes from God, for God cannot be tempted with evil and neither does he tempt anyone.

In Luke Chapter 4 Verses 1 to 13 we are told what happened to Jesus after he had been baptised in the river Jordan.

Jesus was full of the Holy Spirit when he returned from the Jordan and was led by the Spirit into the desert, where he was tempted by the devil for forty days. During those days he did not eat anything and was very hungry when they were ended.

The devil said to him: If you are the Son of God, tell this stone to become a loaf of bread.

Jesus answered him: It has been written, Man shall not live only on bread.

And taking him up high, he showed him all the kingdoms of the earth all at the same time and the devil said to him: I will give you authority over all this and all the wealth and splendour will be yours, because this has become mine and I can give it to whomever I wish; If you, therefore, will worship me then all this will be yours.

And answering him, Jesus said: It has been written, You shall worship the Lord your God and him only shall you serve.

And he led him to Jerusalem and set him upon the gable of the temple roof and said to him: If you are the Son of God, throw yourself down now; for it has been written: He will give his angels orders about you, to protect you and they will lift you up in their hands so that you do not even hurt your foot against a stone.

And Jesus answered him saying: It has been said, You shall not tempt the Lord your God.

And having finished every temptation, the devil left him for a while.

These verses of scripture clearly show:
1. That it was the Holy Spirit who led Jesus into the desert but that it was the devil who tempted him, not God.
2. That if the Son of God can be tempted, then so can we, no-one is immune from temptation.
3. Just because we are tempted, like Jesus we do not have to give in to it.
4. In the Gospel of John Chapter 10 Verse 30 Jesus said:

    I and my Father are one.

    So when the devil tempted Jesus, he was tempting God, which is why James confirms in Verse 13 that: *God cannot be tempted with evil.*

    God is good, He is Just, He is righteous, that is His very nature and He can never do anything that would contravene it.
5. Jesus used the bible to answer the devil:

    Verse 4. It has been written, Man shall not live only on bread. (Deuteronomy Chapter 8 Verse 3).

> Verse 8. It has been written, You shall worship the Lord your God and him only shall you serve. (Deuteronomy Chapter 6 Verse 13).
>
> Verse 12. : It has been said, You shall not tempt the Lord your God. (Deuteronomy Chapter 6 Verse 16).

Jesus both knew and could quote the book of Deuteronomy; how many of us could do that today?

When was the last time you actually read the book of Deuteronomy?

Do you know where it is in the bible?

Yes, I know it is not an easy book to get to grips with but surely if Jesus found it essential in fighting temptation, then so should we!

14. But each man is tempted when he is drawn away from God by the lusts of his own heart which he finds enticing;

15. So lust then, having been conceived gives birth to sin and sin, having been fully formed, brings about death.

The word 'lust' today normally has strong sexual connotations but James uses the word in Verse 14 to describe the extremely strong longings or desires that we might have which will eventually entice us to act in a way which is outside the will or law of God or might lead us to absent ourselves from the fellowship of other believers.

So temptation gives birth to lust (or wrongful desires), lust gives birth to sin and sin will eventually separate us from the will of God, which brings death.

The term 'gives birth' is a warning to us that a small error or misdemeanour, if not corrected, can lead to an out of control monster that will wreck lives.

There is absolutely no point in asking God to help you overcome a sin, such as watching pornography or gambling, when deep down in your heart, you know you really enjoy doing it.

You have to ask God to change your heart's desires, so that you stop enjoying it and then after you stop enjoying it; it becomes something you do not want to do anymore and you can ask for help in giving it up completely.

16. Do not go astray (be deceived), my beloved brothers.

In Luke Chapter 21 Verse 8 Jesus warned us:

Beware, in-case you should be deceived; for many will come in my name saying: 'I AM (Jesus),' and: 'The time has drawn near.' Do not go after them.

Most of us enjoy a 'Magic Show' where a magician pulls a rabbit out of a hat or saws a lady in half. I remember when a magician visited my school when I was very young and how he wonderfully produced a silver coin from behind my ear and how annoyed I was that he wouldn't let me keep it; it was from my ear after all!

But a 'Magic Show' is after all, just that, a show! What James is warning us about in verse 14 and what Jesus warned his disciples about were people who pretended to be something that they were not.

I remember that while I was working in the City of London in around 1966/67 I received a letter from a very nice man in Nigeria who pretended to be my friend and benefactor. He informed me that he had discovered that I had somehow inherited a small fortune in Nigeria and that if I were to send him a cheque for a certain sum of money that he, out of the goodness of his heart, would put the wheels in motion to secure this small fortune for me.

I showed the letter to my two colleagues, who were a lot older, wiser and more experienced in the ways of the world than I was who suggested that I file the letter in the wastepaper basket, which is what I did.

How sad that fifty years later, this same scam is still being worked by fraudsters on un-suspecting, vulnerable people all over the world.

Someone once said to me, 'If something seems too good to be true, that is probably because it is!'

How sad it is that down through the ages thousands of Christian believers have been led astray by fraudsters, which is why it is so important to know your bible for yourself and to be in fellowship with a body of believers who are truly grounded in the word and love of God and are not easily led astray.

17. Every act of good giving and every perfect gift comes down from above, from the Father of lights, with whom there is neither variation nor shadow of turning.

Two friends were walking along a cliff path somewhere on the south coast of England one wet Autumn day when a sudden gust of wind caught the umbrella that one of them was holding and lifted the man and his umbrella up into the air and over the cliff edge. As the man fell he let go of the umbrella and eventually managed to grab hold of a bush that was growing out from the face of the cliff.

"I can't see you," his friend called out, "are you all right?"

"Of course I am not all right, I have just been blown over a cliff and have hurt my left arm and am holding onto this small bush with just one hand," the man replied.

"How far down the cliff have you fallen?" asked the friend.

"About thirty feet," (ten metres) he replied.

To cut a long story short, the friend phoned the emergency services on his mobile phone who answered immediately and promised to send assistance.

The first to arrive were the local Fire Service who spoke to the man through a loud hailer and told him that they were going to send a fireman down on a rope ladder to rescue him.

"No need," the man replied, "I have just prayed about my situation and have asked God to rescue me, so you can go back to your fire-station, but thank you for coming."

The firemen were wondering what to do when they suddenly got a telephone call telling them to go back to town to deal with a fire at a local bakery, so they left the cliff edge and returned to town.

Next to arrive was the local lifeboat who shouted up to the man that he should let go of the bush and drop into the sea as there were no rocks under where he was hanging and the water was deep just there and they would rescue him from the water.

"No need," the man replied, "I have just prayed about my situation and have asked God to rescue me, so you can go back to your lifeboat-station, but thank you for coming."

The lifeboat men were wondering what to do when they suddenly got a telephone call telling them to go back to harbour to help in the rescue of a young lad who was drifting out to sea in his canoe, so they also left the scene.

Last to arrive was an Air Sea Rescue helicopter with a man dangling from a ladder underneath it, but they too were turned away by the man who said that he was waiting for God to rescue him.

An hour or so later the small bush came away from the cliff and the man fell into the sea and was drowned.

When he reached the Pearly gates of heaven he was ready to give the gatekeeper a piece of his mind for letting him die.

"What do you mean we let you die?" said the gatekeeper. "We sent you the Fire Brigade and the lifeboat and even called out the Ait Sea Rescue for you and you sent them all away. Just because we didn't dispatch an angel to pluck you off the cliff face and fly you home, which is what you were hoping for, doesn't mean that God ignored your prayer."

Whilst it is up to each individual to decide what they are going to pray, it is God who decides the most suitable answer in response to that prayer.

God has a thousand and one ways in which to bless his children so take the opportunity to be thankful to God, as well as to anyone he uses to bless you each and every time it happens and remember that even at work during a hectic day, you have the opportunity to thank him even if it is just for a cup of coffee or a mug of tea.

18. Having resolved (what to do), he brought us forth (gave birth to us) by the word of truth, that we should be a kind of first-fruits of his creatures.

In Verse 18 James carries on the theme of the Father's gifts to us by reminding the readers of his letter that the gift of 'the word of truth' was a conscious decision by God in order that those who accepted Jesus Christ as Lord and Saviour would be 'born again' or 'brought forth'.

Right at the start of the Gospel of John we are told about Jesus:
Chapter 1
1. In the beginning was the *Word*, and the *Word* was with God and the *Word* was God.
2. The same was in the beginning with God.
3. All things were made through him; and without him, nothing was made which has been made.
4. In him was life and the life was the light of men.
5. And the light shines in the darkness but the darkness has not comprehended it.

14. And the *Word* was made flesh and dwelt among us, and we beheld his glory, the glory of the one and only Son of the Father, full of grace and *truth*.
17. Because the law was given through Moses, but grace and *truth* came through Jesus Christ.

From my understanding of this verse, 'the word of truth' is a direct reference to Jesus and to his life and ministry and how Jesus is God's gift to a fallen world.

In 1 Peter Chapter 1 Verse 23 the apostle states quite clearly that 'we have been born again by the word of God which lives forever.'

And writing to the Colossians Paul says in Chapter 1 Verse 5:
Because of the hope which is stored up for you in heaven, which you heard about before in 'the word of the truth' of the gospel which has come to you.

According to my dictionary first-fruits are the fruit (or plant) which ripens first or it can be understood to mean the first results, products or profits from an undertaking, so when James says : *that we should be a kind of first-fruits of his creatures* it would appear that he is talking about himself and the other early Christians who were just the start of the harvest of souls that would follow in their footsteps in the years to come.

But surely the harvest might well continue long after we are dead and gone so each one of us should do what we can to make sure that those who follow us have the same opportunities that we had to come to know Jesus as their Lord and Saviour.

19. Understand this, my beloved brothers, let every man be swift to hear, slow to speak and slow to get angry;

In Mark Chapter 9 Verse 7 we are told that on the mount of transfiguration the three disciples Peter, John and his brother James heard the voice of God say: This is my beloved Son. *Hear* Him!

God tells us through Isaiah the prophet in Chapter 55 Verse 11: My word shall not return to me void (empty, useless), but will accomplish exactly what I want it to.

Right at the start of the book of Proverbs in Chapter 1 Verse 8 we are told: My son, hear the instruction of your father.

Most of us came to a saving knowledge of the Lord Jesus through hearing the word of God, be it in a church or a Christian meeting somewhere, or on the TV or radio or a tape or CD or suchlike or perhaps through the prompting of the Holy Spirit while reading the bible at home.

As believers we should never stop listening to what God has to say to us.

In particular, I believe it is important that the bible be read out loud, so that people have an opportunity to hear it, at Christian gatherings. I feel really saddened when attending some fellowships and find that the bible is never read out loud during the entire service.

It is amazing how wise some people can appear to be when they say nothing but gently nod in agreement to what a speaker is saying and if they do say a few words, a quietly spoken, "That is so true, very well put." can appear to be the words of a sage.

On the other hand, a person who speaks without thinking and makes comments about subjects he knows nothing about is very quickly written off as a loud-mouth and a fool.

Proverbs Chapter 14 Verse 17 warns us: He who gets angry very quickly, acts foolishly!
And Chapter 22 Verse 24 advises us: Do not strike up a friendship with an angry man.

Someone who cannot control their anger is a liability to themselves and to everyone they are associated with.
If you have a 'short fuse' then ask God to lengthen it for you and to teach you how to exercise 'self-control', which is, of course, one of the 'Fruits of the Spirit' as stated in Galatians Chapter 5 Verses 22 and 23:
But the fruit of the spirit is love, joy, peace, patience, kindness, goodness, faithfulness, gentleness, *self-control*; against such (fruit) as these, there is no law.

20. For the anger of a man does not work the righteousness of God (does not cause the righteousness of God to function).

Mark Chapter 3 Verse 17 informs us that the two sons of Zebedee, James and John, were given the nickname Boanerges (Sons of Thunder) by Jesus which has always been understood to mean that they were two 'angry young men'.
This is demonstrated in Luke Chapter 9 Verses 52 to 56:
And he sent messengers ahead of him and they went into a Samaritan village in order to prepare for him, but they did not receive him, because he was travelling to Jerusalem.

On seeing this, the disciples James and John said: Lord, would you like us to command fire to come down from heaven and destroy them?

But turning, he (Jesus) rebuked them. And they went to another village.

You can just imagine Jesus looking at the two brothers, shaking his head and saying, "What is wrong with the pair of you?"

In Ephesians Chapter 6 Verses 10 to 17 Paul talks about the 'Armour of God' likening the role of a Christian to that of a soldier in the Roman army. A soldier has to be disciplined and self-controlled; he cannot break ranks and act on his own just because he has got upset or angry about something.

In verses 13 and 14 Paul says: Therefore take for yourselves, the whole armour of God, in order that you may be able to resist the evil which comes against you each day and after everything has happened to you, to stand.

Stand therefore, tightening the belt of truth round your waist and putting on the *breastplate of righteousness.*

For the 'righteousness of God' to work in our lives we have to be under his command and not allow anger, frustration, irritation and the like to blur our judgement and control our actions.

21. Therefore, putting away all filthiness and the unnecessary abundance of evil, receive with meekness the implanted word, which is able to save your souls.

We cannot change what we have done or thought in the past, but we can make a conscious decision to clean up our act in the future. There is no place in the fellowship of believers for those who wish to continue with their sinful ways after they have accepted Jesus as Lord and Saviour.

In Paul's letter to Titus, Chapter 2 Verses 11 to 13 he tells us that the grace of God teaches us that we should keep ourselves from ungodliness and worldly lusts and that we should live righteous, sober and godly lives as we wait patiently for the Lord to come again.

In Romans Chapter 6 Paul discusses why a Christian should keep from sinning. In Verses 1 and 2 he says: What do you think then? Is it O.K. for us to continue sinning so that God's grace may continue to abound (act in our lives). Certainly not! (Of course it isn't!) How can we who are believers and have died to sin continue to live steeped or immersed in sinful ways and habits!

And in Verse 12 he warns us: Not to let sin reign over (have control of) our bodies and not to be subject to sinful lusts, desires or ways of behaving.

And how can we know what is sin and what is not sin?

We can start by reading and digesting the first five books of the Old Testament, the Pentateuch as it is called and then work our way through the New Testament, asking the Holy Spirit to interpret those bits which we find difficult to understand and to enable us to accept and receive the word into our hearts and minds.

In case you think that the Old Testament is no longer of any relevance or importance to Christians, remember what Jesus stated in Matthew Chapter 5 Verses 17 and 18:

Do not think that I came to destroy the law or the prophets, I did not come as a destroyer, but as a fulfiller.

For truly I say to you, until heaven and earth have passed away, not one word or the slightest pen stroke (punctuation mark), shall pass away (be removed) from the law, until everything has come to pass (as my Father has ordained).

22. And (what is more), become doers of the word and not just hearers, otherwise you would be misleading yourselves.

23. Because if anyone is a hearer of the word and not a doer, he is like a man who looks at his own face in a mirror,

24. And having looked at himself, goes away and immediately forgets what he looked like.

At the tender age of five or six I was on a Sunday School outing at Littlehampton, which is a seaside resort on the south coast of England, when I wandered off from where my parents were sitting and managed to get myself lost.

I knew I was lost but as this had happened to me before I was not overly stressed about it and knew that there was a 'Lost Children' chalet somewhere on the beach. Eventually a nice lady took my hand and led me to the chalet where I duly gave my name and the name of the Sunday School I was with and an announcement was made over the tannoy (loudspeaker system) that a little boy, by my name, was at the Lost Children Chalet and would his parents please come and collect him.

In due course my parents turned up and identified me as their son and I identified them as my parents and off we went together back to their deck chairs.

Now imagine if my parents had been hearers of the word and not doers of the word as well. They might have chatted about the fact that it was their son who was at the Lost Children Chalet and how many times they had told me that day not to wander off from them. They may have commented about how well or badly the announcer spoke and whether the system was as good as the one at Ramsgate, which they had listened to when I had got lost there once before.

They might have made detailed notes in a little book about the announcement or recorded the date in a special diary kept specifically for the purpose but if they had not done what the announcer instructed, i.e. got up from their deck chairs and walked to the Lost Children Chalet, my life's story could have turned out a lot different from what it has.

I find it interesting that James must have had the same problems in the early church that we still have today i.e. people who are great listeners and are always asking for 'more teaching' but seem incapable of putting into practice what they have already heard.

We joke about the 'eternal student'! People who go from school to college, to university, to another college and then another university who are constantly seeking more and more qualifications that they never put to good use; but unfortunately there are many people in our churches who do something similar and from what James said in Verses 23 and 24 it would appear that he did not have a lot of time for them.

25. But the person who having looked into the perfect law of freedom (which sets us free) and continues in doing this, not being a forgetful hearer, but a doer of the work (of what it says), this person shall be blessed in what he undertakes.

At the start of his ministry Jesus returned to Nazareth and Luke Chapter 4 Verses 16 to 21 tell us what happened:

And he came to Nazareth, where he was brought up, and he entered the synagogue on the Sabbath day, as was his normal habit and he stood up to read the scriptures.

And he was given a roll of the prophet Isaiah and opening the roll he found the place where it was written:

'The Spirit of the Lord is upon me, for which reason he has anointed me to evangelise the poor, he has sent me to proclaim *freedom* to those who are captives and to those who are blind – sight, to set free and send on their way those who have been crushed (in spirit);

To proclaim the acceptable year of the Lord.'

And having closed the roll he returned it to the attendant and sat down; and everyone in the synagogue was looking at him.

And he started speaking to them saying: Today this scripture has been fulfilled in your hearing.

Right at the start of his teaching ministry Jesus announced that he was here to set free, those who were captive to sin.

James tells us that as we continue to hear and read the word of God and to put it into practice in our daily lives that God will bless us in whatever we undertake.

This blessing is not limited to our church activities but to every aspect of our lives which we open up to Him. Our homes, our marriages our jobs even our hobbies can be blessed by God if we put into practice what we have heard.

26. If anyone thinks of himself as being religious and does not have control of his own tongue then he is just deceiving himself and his religion is futile and fruitless.

27. Religion which God the Father considers to be clean and undefiled is this, to visit orphans and widows when they are distressed and to keep oneself unspotted (untainted and uncontaminated) from the world.

My copy of Cruden's Complete Concordance – Student Edition was printed in London in 1769 and was based on The King James Version of the Bible and lists only two references to the word 'religious' the first being Acts Chapter 13 Verse 43, which tells us that: religious proselytes followed Paul and James Chapter 1 Verse 26, as above.

The word 'religion' has only five references, one in the book of Acts, two in Galatians and two in James, as above, so the concept of a person having a religion and of being religious is very closely linked to the New Testament.

My dictionary has several definitions of the word 'religion' as follows:

The belief in (worship of or obedience to) a divine, supernatural power or being.

The practice of sacred rituals, ceremonies and rites.

Something of overwhelming, life controlling, importance to a person such as work – family – football!

So a person who is 'religious' is therefore, someone who is putting his religion into effect which need have absolutely nothing to do with Christianity.

In Matthew Chapter 23 Verses 1 to 36 Jesus tells the scribes and Pharisees exactly what he thinks of them and although he does not actually use the term 'religious fanatics', that is how we would think of them today. People who are so obsessed by what they believe and how they think things should be done, that they lose all sense of proportion and of what Jesus would say and do in their places.

James is not saying that there is anything wrong with religion or with being religious, provided one's religion is based on the Gospel of Jesus and the fruit of one's religious activity is honouring and pleasing to God; such as helping those in need and in living a clean and untainted life.

That concludes Chapter One and leaves us asking James a lot of question as to exactly what sort of religious activity would be considered acceptable to God which he himself answers, in part anyway, in Chapter Two.

DISCUSSION SUBJECTS FOR CHAPTER ONE

1. Why do you think it is important for all Christians to demonstrate humility?

2. Which part of 'taking up your cross daily' do you find most difficult?

3. Looking back, which past trials have shaped your character for the better?

4. When would you find a bit of extra wisdom most useful?

5. Give an example of being 'two minded' about something.

6. In what way would a man be blessed who remained faithful throughout a trial?

7. What 'good gift' has God given you when you were not expecting it?

8. Which 'Fruit of the Spirit' would you most like to see developing in your life?

9. How would you help someone who is easily angered?

10. What worldly things would you advise a young Christian to stay away from?

Chapter Four

COMMENTARY ON THE BOOK OF JAMES

Chapter Two

1. My brothers, having faith in our glorious Lord Jesus Christ you must treat everyone equally (and not show more respect to one person than another).

2. For if a well dressed man should come into your meeting with a gold ring on his finger along with a poor man in shabby clothing,

3. And you look at the man wearing the expensive clothes and say, 'here's a nice seat, why don't you sit down here' and to the poor man say, 'you can stand over there or sit here on the floor by me':

4. Have you not shown discrimination among yourselves and become guilty of making judgements based on evil thoughts (wrong standards).

I would estimate that in the sixty years that I have been listening to sermons in church that the subject of 'discrimination' has to be one of the least discussed/preached on subjects that I can think of.

Another subject which is almost as unpopular is 'respect' so for James to bring these two matters up at the start of the second chapter of his letter would imply that there was a serious problem in the early church which he wanted to bring out into the open.

Whilst, personally speaking, I do not think that 'Society' at large is any more discriminatory today than it was sixty years ago, I do feel that we have become less respectful in the 21st Century than we were in the previous one but since James' letter is aimed at the early church I will concentrate on how these two matters are manifest in the church today and what we should be doing about them.

RESPECT

When we show respect towards another person we are demonstrating an attitude of deference or admiration or regard or consideration towards them. We are behaving in a way that showed we had regard for their feelings or sensitivities or frailties or needs.

One of the ways in which we have become less respectful in the 21st Century inside our churches is punctuality for services/meetings.

I am sure that if we had an audience booked with the Queen or the Prime Minister we would make sure that we were there on time as a sign of our respect for them and the fear that we might lose our slot if we are late.

Every time we attend a church service/meeting we are having an audience with the King of Kings and Lord of Lords and yet some people seem to hold our God in such contempt that they turn up late week after week. I have been in a church where it became such a problem that the services started five minutes late each week to accommodate these people, who promptly started to turn up ten minutes late instead.

As a young man my timekeeping was not always spot on but if I did happen to arrive late and found that the service had started, out of respect for the other worshippers, I waited until the first hymn and then went in as quietly as I could and sat at the back of the church so as not to disturb them. Today people seem to have no respect for other worshippers and just come in when they want to, no matter what is going on in the service and seemingly, making as much noise and causing as much confusion as they want to.

I mentioned above that in demonstrating respect that we should show regard for other people's frailties and needs and that this might take the form of helping the infirm to their seat, providing toys or writing material for children and not having the volume of the worship group turned up so high that it hurts people's ears or leaves them with a headache.

In mentioning worship, the choice of songs to sing should cater for the whole congregation and not just the age group of those who are leading. We who are over seventy grew up on the old hymns of Charles Wesley, John Ellerton, John Newton and the like and just love the words and music and would be really blessed if we sang some of them occasionally, whilst understanding that the younger members of the congregation would not want to sing too many of them at any one time.

In Ephesians Chapter 5 Verses 22 to 33 Paul talks to believers about the relationship between a man and a woman in marriage and ends with the statement:
Nevertheless let every one of you understand, that each of you must love your wife as yourself and every wife must see to it, that she *respects* her husband.

When a wife loses respect for her husband and is openly disrespectful towards him, that marriage is doomed because every time she is disrespectful, something inside of him dies.

I understand that we will probably not be going back to the days when gentlemen tipped their hats to ladies in the street and seats were offered on public transport to those with a greater need than the occupant but surely in our churches we can encourage a respectful attitude between members, both, young and old and those in the middle.

DISCRIMINATION
The unfair treatment of a person based on prejudice.

In discussing this subject I should start off with the premise on which I will be making my comments and that is:
'We all like to be with people (are comfortable with people) who we consider to be just like us.'

Growing up in South London and going to State schools and the local church, virtually everyone I associated with came from a similar background to me. Some of my friends and schoolmates were a bit wealthier than we were and some were a bit poorer, but by and large we were all pretty much the same and I was blissfully unaware that being 'working class' made me a member of the lowest class in society.

I then started work and my first job was with a firm of City Stockbrokers where I very quickly found out that the 'Class System' in Britain was alive and well.

The vast majority of my peers came from 'middle class' backgrounds and apart from wearing more expensive suits than myself and having shirts with detachable collars, they were not too different from me and we got on well together.

After a while I was allowed to visit other departments where the 'upper class' and 'aristocracy' worked and I found this to be a completely different kettle of fish.

Now I have to be honest and say that the vast majority of people I came across were friendly, polite and helpful but there were definitely some who gave me the impression that I was too low a being for them to acknowledge, except by way of making unkind remarks about the way I dressed and spoke.

Discrimination is not just about racial differences it is about any difference that makes us prejudiced towards another human being, no matter how small or large that difference might be, but as we make the effort to get to know people who we, at first glance, considered to be different, we often come to realise that they are a lot more like us than we might originally have thought possible.

Having said that, what form can discrimination take in the church of the 21st Century?

The one that James pointed out in his letter i.e. poor man/rich man is still alive and well but I would say that we are a lot better at handling this than we used to be. This may be due in part to the fact that in my youth most people used to put on their 'Sunday Best' to go to church, so anyone who did not own a 'Sunday Best' stood out like a sore thumb whereas nowadays a lot of people do not bother to dress up to go to church but wear whatever comes to hand.

Again I would say that most churches handle racial differences quite well and although most people are naturally curious about someone in their midst that they do not know or who is obviously different to them, generally speaking this curiosity does not lead to discrimination.

I was fortunate enough to attend a church in Shanghai a few years ago where my companion and I were the only two Westerners present and whilst many in the congregation took the opportunity for a sly look at us when they could, there was certainly no hint of discrimination and everyone was extremely friendly and helpful.

The differences of the sexes can also lead to problems in a church but whereas sixty years ago women were very much expected to take a back seat, apart from children and women's work, these days they are an integral part of all aspects of the life of the church, but as in all church matters, decisions should be made based on a person's suitability for a post, after much prayer, rather than just trying to achieve a gender balance.

The one area where I believe a lot of churches have taken a backward step in regard to discrimination is age, particularly old age.

In my youth the average age of our deacons and elders would have been around sixty and most of them would have gone to be with their Lord by the time they were seventy.

Today most of us can expect to live well into our eighties and nineties and lead active lives certainly into our eighties.

If we wish to attend a church which primarily caters for the elderly, then we might still find ourselves in a leadership position and all that entails, for as long as we care to fulfil the role but if we wish to attend a church which covers all ages, from the very young to the very old, then if we are over sixty five we might find ourselves excluded from leadership roles.

Whilst there is a need to train and encourage the next generation in order to safeguard the future of the church, it seems a shame to lose the experience and dedication of the older generation and to discriminate against them, somewhere there has to be a balance so that we can encourage the one without alienating the other.

5. Listen to me, my beloved brothers; has not God chosen the poor of this world to be rich in faith and heirs of the kingdom which he promised those that love him?

In Luke Chapter 18 Verses 18 to 25 we have the story about the rich ruler who came to Jesus and asked:

What must I do to inherit eternal life?

and in verses 24 and 25 Jesus makes the comment:

How seldom the ones having property go into the kingdom of God; it is easier for a camel to enter through the eye of a needle, than a rich man to enter into the kingdom of God.

How stark a comment is that?

There is no ambiguity in what Jesus said about being rich in the things of this world which is why he warned his listeners in Luke Chapter 12 Verse 34:

For where your treasure is, there your heart will be also.

We live in a materialistic world where we are bombarded throughout the day with advertisements telling us that we need something and that we should not stop until we get it.

If being wealthy or prosperous or famous is such a wonderful thing to achieve, how is it that so many people who have achieved these things appear to live such sad, broken lives.

How often do we notice in our churches that as members of the congregation become wealthier that their attendance at church seems to drop off? Whether it be a morning's round of golf with the boss or an important client or just sleeping in after a late night out, as sure as day follows night, lack of commitment at church seems to follow worldly success.

Hebrews Chapter 11 talks about 'Faith' and starts with a definition in verse 1:

Now faith is the reality of things hoped for, the proof of things not seen.

So why should this 'faith' be present in the poor to a greater degree than it is in the rich?

Could it be because they rely on God to provide for their needs rather than themselves or their rich friends and family? When you haven't got enough to eat and you have no other hope of getting food, then it is easy to start trusting in a divine being that might answer your prayers and when he does, you start to trust him in other aspects of your life as well.

In Luke Chapter 18 Verse 17 Jesus said:
Truly I tell you, whoever does not receive the kingdom of God as a child, shall not be able to enter into it.

For those of us who were fortunate enough to accept Jesus as our Lord and Saviour as children, we will remember that it was not a difficult thing to do. There were no deep meaningful discussions about the meaning of life and pre-destination and the like, something inside us simply told us that it was the right thing to do and when we were told that Jesus would always be with us and would always love us and watch over us, we believed and accepted this as true from the people we loved and trusted.

Be careful of what you wish for and think twice before you ask God for things which could, if allowed to get out of hand, spoil your relationship with him and don't be afraid to ask yourself:
Where is my treasure found today?

6. But you dishonour the poor man. Is it not the rich men who oppress you and drag you into court?

7. Do they not blaspheme the good name by which you have been called?

James probably had a particular instance in mind when he pointed out that it was not the poor who had oppressed them and had taken them to court but the rich. Taking legal proceedings against someone or some organization has always been an expensive option and not one open to poor people.

I recall an instance many years ago when a local newspaper interviewed me about a canoeing expedition I had led with some of the youth in our church which had gone slightly wrong but everything had turned out O.K. in the end and a good time had been had by all.

The headline in the newspaper read, 'Up the wrong creek without a paddle' and gave the impression that the expedition was a disaster from start to finish and that I was a complete idiot.

As you can imagine I was pretty upset about the article and spoke to one of the elders in my church about it who suggested that I put it down to experience and move on with my life as these things were quickly forgotten and legal consultations were prohibitively expensive; which is exactly what I did.

I think that one of the saddest aspects of modern life compared to sixty years ago is the way that blasphemy has become so widespread in everyday conversation.

People who have never used the 'f' word in their life and would protest most vehemently if someone else did, happily blaspheme with every conversation they have, whether it be face to face or electronically.

In a work situation, particularly where you are the junior, it is very hard to make a stand against blasphemy but in my experience, where I have had the courage to say something, I found most people to be understanding and to be more careful of their language when I was present. But having made a stand, I had to be a lot more careful of my own language and subjects of conversation to make sure that I was not on the receiving end of a rebuke from them.

8. If indeed you are fulfilling the royal law according to scripture, 'you shall love your neighbour as yourself;' you are doing well:

9. But if you are showing discrimination with regard to people, you are committing a sin and will be convicted by the law as transgressors (lawbreakers).

Leviticus Chapter 19 Verse 18 says:
You shall not take vengeance against the children of your people or even bear them a grudge, but *you shall love your neighbour as yourself.*

In Matthew Chapter 19 Verse 19 Jesus quoted this verse when he answered the question posed by the rich young ruler who wanted to know what he had to do to inherit eternal life and again in Lukes account of an expert in the law asking the same question of Jesus in Chapter 10 Verses 25 to 28 the expert quoted the verse at Jesus when he said:

You should love the Lord your God with all your heart and with all your soul and with all your strength and with all your mind *and your neighbour as yourself.*

To which Jesus replied:

You have answered correctly, do this and you will live

In Romans Chapter 13 Verses 8 to 10 Paul talks about the power of love and says in Verse 8 that :

The person who loves another has fulfilled the law.

and in Verse 9 after listing some of the commandments he concludes with the statement that:

All are summed up in the one commandment, 'You shall love your neighbour as yourself.'

which is repeated again in Galatians Chapter 5 Verse 14.

It is small wonder then, that James' calls this particular commandment the 'Royal' law. It is the law we should put first in our thinking before we start to understand and consider all the other laws which affect our relationship with other people, some of which are mentioned by Paul in Romans Chapter 13 Verse 9.

James tells us that if we are keeping the 'Royal' law that we are doing well, which means every time we break it, that we are doing badly! This thought should make us bite our tongues the next time we are about to make a rude or sarcastic comment to someone or we are on the verge of saying something unpleasant about someone behind their back. Remember, just because everyone else is doing it, does not make it O.K. for us to do it too.

Which is probably why James gives his readers a reminder in Verse 9 that: *discrimination with regard to people* is a sin.

That is not to say that we should not discriminate (make choices) about other things. I choose to wear a particular brand of shirt when I can, as I find them particularly comfortable, but others might choose to wear another brand.
I choose to wear a particular type of hat when I am playing lawn bowls compared to most other bowlers as I need to protect the back of my neck from the sun and I like to watch a particular type of film compared to some other people.

There is nothing wrong or sinful in the actual act of making choices, but the things we choose to do may in themselves be sinful, but when we show *discrimination with regard to people,* no matter how insignificant that discrimination might be, we are actually committing a sin.

10. For he who keeps the whole law, yet stumbles in just one thing, has become guilty of breaking all of it.

11. For the one who said, 'Do not commit adultery', also said, 'Do not murder', now if you do not commit adultery but you do murder, you have become a transgressor of the law (a lawbreaker).

LAW

A rule or set of rules legally or constitutionally put in place to punish those who act in a way which is contrary to the conventions of society.

LAW-BREAKER

Anyone who breaks the law.

SIN

Any offence in breach of the known will of God or any breach of any law or principle which is regarded as embodying his will.

Romans Chapter 6 Verse 23A informs us that:
The wages of sin is death.

That is surely very clear and cannot be misinterpreted, no matter how harsh we personally consider that statement to be.

It never struck me as fair that a person who may have lived the perfect 'sin-free' life but in their final hour on this earth did some minor thing like swear at the postman for kicking a favourite pot plant over, should, for that one sin, be sent to hell.

That is, perhaps, why James points out that being good, or at least better than everyone else, does not guarantee us a place in heaven, because just one small sin is enough to separate us from God.

You might console yourself in thinking that since James picked murder and adultery as his two examples, both very serious breaches of the law which you have probably not committed, that you are O.K. but in Matthew Chapter 5 Verses 33 to 37 Jesus clearly tells us that swearing (bad language and blasphemy) is wrong and he concludes by saying in verse 37:
But let your communication be 'yes and yes' and 'no and no', for whatever you say more than this is 'evil'.

Something most of us have done on many occasions.

Thanks goodness, therefore, that the other half of Romans Chapter 6 Verse 23 tells us:
The gift of God is eternal life in Christ Jesus our Lord.

When we break God's law we can receive forgiveness through his Son but because we, as believers, know that to be true, it does not mean that we should give up on trying to keep his law.
Even though we might break his law on a regular basis we should never make a conscious decision to just ignore it in our daily lives with the intention of getting right with him again the next time we happen to go to church, that would be hypocrisy of the worst kind.

12. So, you should speak and behave as though you were about to be judged by a law of freedom:

James is here reminding his readers of what he said to them in Chapter 1 verse 25 i.e. Jesus has set you free from any hold the world might have on you. You do not have to live your life under the rules or expectations that the world places on you but you are free to live as an adopted son or daughter of God and you are no longer a slave to sin.

In Galatians Chapter 3 Verses 1 to 14 Paul remonstrates with the church at Galatia for going back to a worldly perspective and lifestyle rather than living in the freedom which Christ had given them.

He starts in Verse 1 by saying:

O foolish Galatians who has bewitched you that you should not obey the truth?

And he asks in Verse 3:

Are you really so foolish? Having begun in the Spirit, are you being made perfect in the flesh?

You can almost imagine the incredulity he must have felt when he wrote those verses but they are a warning to all of us today that we should not give up the freedom which we have in Christ in order to please man or a set of rules which some super self-appointed modern-day apostle has burdened us with.

In Verse 12 James warns us that believers will be judged on how we have lived and behaved in regard to the freedom which Christ bought for us with his sacrifice on the cross.

13. For judgement will be without mercy for the person who has not shown mercy; mercy exults (is joyfully triumphant) over judgement.

In Matthew Chapter 6 Verses 9 to 13 Jesus taught his disciples how to pray:

9. Therefore you should pray in this way; Our Father who is in the heavens, may your name be hallowed (reverenced and holy);

10. Let your kingdom come, let your will be done on earth as it is in heaven.

11. Give us this day our daily bread;

12. And forgive us our debts as indeed we forgive our debtors;

13. And do not bring us into temptation, but rescue us from evil.

And in Verses 14 and 15 he went on to say:

If you forgive men their trespasses (when they have sinned against you) then your heavenly Father will also forgive you.

However, if you do not forgive men their trespasses then neither will your heavenly Father forgive you your trespasses.

Jesus told his disciples in Matthew Chapter 5 Verse 7:
Blessed are the merciful, for they will obtain mercy.

So forgiving others is not an option for Christians, it is a command which we are expected to follow, no matter how difficult the circumstances appear to be.

In my opinion, this is the most difficult command in the whole bible for us Christians to keep.

I can love the Lord my God with all my heart and with all of my strength and with all of my mind, I can keep well away from stealing and murdering and committing adultery but forgiving that person who has wronged me is a real struggle, particularly if that wrong has changed my whole life or the lives of those I love.

Without the example of Christ and all the teaching he left us on this subject, I do not think I would ever be able, in my own strength, to forgive others.

After Jesus had been betrayed, tormented, spat upon, tortured, scourged and nailed to a cross and left to die, he could still pray out loud, as recorded in Luke Chapter 23 Verse 34:

Father, forgive them; for they do not know what they are doing.

When Jesus invited us to follow him (Luke Chapter 9 Verse 23) he did not give us the right to choose which bits of him we could follow and which bits we could ignore, so just as he forgave those who had wronged him, he now expects us to forgive those who have wronged us.

James Chapter 2 Verses 14 to 26

In the remaining verses of Chapter 2 James is talking about the practicalities of being a Christian and is not bringing into doubt the assertion made by Paul in Ephesians Chapter 2 Verses 8 and 9 when he proclaimed:

For by grace you have been saved, through faith; and this not of yourselves; it is the gift of God; not of works, in case anyone should boast.

We are saved through our faith in the Lord Jesus and what James is stating in the following verses is about how we should be demonstrating that faith to the world and the difference it should make to the way we live our lives.

14. What profit is there my brothers, if anyone says that they have faith but does not have works (actions to demonstrate that faith)? Do you think that faith like that can save him?

In John Chapter 8 Verse 12 we are told:
Once again Jesus spoke to them saying: I am the light of the world; the one who follows me will not walk in darkness, but shall have the light of life.

As Christians we believe that the Holy Ghost dwells in us and since Father, Son and Holy Ghost are one, Jesus dwells in us. So if Jesus is the 'light of the world' then we are the 'light of the world' in his place which makes Luke Chapter 11 Verse 33 very pertinent for us:
No-one having lit a lamp, places it in a secret place, or under a box, but puts it on a lamp stand, so that anyone who enters may see the light.

We Christians, therefore, can't stop being 'the light' and shining out into a dark world, if only by the way that we live and behave. Many millions of people believe in a God and some of those believe that Jesus existed in the flesh and was a special person and some of those might even try and follow his teaching and read his word on a regular basis, but if they are not actually shining out into a dark world and making a difference, James is questioning whether they are truly saved or are simply 'head' believers and not true disciples.

15. If a brother or sister is naked, or is lacking enough food for each day,

16. And one of you says to them, 'Go in peace, be warm (well clothed) and well fed'; but does not give them anything to meet their bodily needs, what is the good of that?

17. In the same way, faith on its own, without works, is dead.

18. But someone will say, 'you have faith and I have works, show me (demonstrate to me) your faith without your works and I will show you (demonstrate to you) my faith, by means of my works.'

There is an expression from where I come from which says, 'words are cheap', which means it is much easier to say something or offer to do something in the future than it is to actually get up and make a difference right now.

How often does someone say at the end of a telephone conversation that they will ring you back, but never do?

Perhaps your car has broken down and you cannot get to an appointment on time and you ring a friend and tell them about your problem and they offer their sincerest sympathy but do not offer to give you a lift, even though they were able to, their sympathy has no value whatsoever.

We cannot respond to every need that exists in our community let alone in the world today but we should be able to point to something in our lives which demonstrates our faith in Jesus.

If non-believers cannot see something different in believers compared to the rest of mankind, why on earth would they want to find out about our Lord and Saviour?

James' statement in Verse 17 is very confronting:
In the same way, faith on its own, without works, is dead.

Let us not forget that James grew up in the same household as Jesus, they were brothers and he would have been used to the way Jesus thought and spoke so when he makes such a 'black and white' statement you can be certain that he is echoing the very thoughts of Jesus himself.

19. Do you believe that there is one God? Good for you; the demons also believe that and shudder.

In verse 19 James is harking back to Verse 14 and the fact that we are not saved by believing in God but only by accepting Jesus as our personal Lord and Saviour.

In Luke Chapter 10 Verses 17 and 18 we have the account given by the seventy two disciples who were sent out to preach the gospel:
And the seventy two returned with joy, saying: Lord, even the demons submit to us, *in your name.*

And he said to them: I witnessed Satan fall, as lightening, from heaven.

Jesus was not surprised that demons submitted to his name.

Luke Chapter 8 Verses 27 to 33 has the account of Jesus being confronted by the demon possessed man after he had crossed the Sea of Galilee and landed in the country of the Gerasenes:

As he got out of the boat and onto the land, he was met by a certain man from the city who had demons and who had not worn clothes or lived in a house for a considerable period of time, but remained among the tombs.

On seeing Jesus he cried out and fell down before him and with a loud voice said: What do we have to do with each other, Jesus, Son of God, most high? I beg you, do not torment me.

For he had commanded the unclean spirit to come out from the man. For many times it had seized him and although he was kept bound with chains and fetters and under guard, he would break free from his bonds and then be driven by the demon into the wilderness.

Jesus questioned him saying: What is your name? And he said Legion, because many demons had entered into him.

And they begged him not to order them to go away into the abyss.

Now there was a herd of many pigs feeding on the mountainside and they begged him that he would allow them to enter into them and he allowed them to.

So the demons came out from the man and entered into the pigs, causing the herd to rush down the steep mountainside and into the lake where they were drowned.

This incident clearly demonstrates that the demons knew exactly who Jesus was and the authority he carried and why they begged him not to send them to the abyss, but into the herd of pigs; which supports James' statement that: *the demons also believe that and shudder.*

20. But are you willing to know (understand, accept), O vain man (you useless, fruitless, insignificant, empty person) that faith without works is barren (it is sterile and unproductive)?

James was obviously concerned that people were not listening to what he had been saying about the need to demonstrate one's faith through one's works and was being very blunt in this verse in order to make sure that everyone was taking this message seriously.

Sometimes being polite and understanding and not wanting to upset people just does not get the message through. Remember what Jesus said to the scribes and Pharisees in Luke Chapter 11 Verses 37 to 54:

Now as he spoke, a Pharisee asked him to dine with him and entering his house, he reclined at table.

But the Pharisee watched and was surprised that he did not first wash before dinner.

And the Lord said to him: Now you Pharisees clean the outside of the cup and the dish but on the inside, you are filled with robbery and wickedness.

Foolish men! Did not the one who made the outside, also make the inside?

Nevertheless, if you give generously and charitably of the things that are within you, everything will be clean to you.

But shame on you Pharisees; because you tithe mint and rue and every herb, but pass by the judgement and love of God; these things you should have done, without passing by the others.

Shame on you Pharisees, because you love the important seats in the synagogues and the greetings in the market-places.

Shame on you, because you are like hidden tombs, that men walk over without knowing.

And answering, one of the lawyers said to him: Teacher, in saying these things, you insult us also.

And he replied: **Shame on you also, you lawyers;** for you burden men with burdens that are difficult to carry, but would not touch one of these burdens with your little finger.

Shame on you, because you build the tombs for the prophets and it was your fathers who killed them.

Therefore you are witnesses (against yourselves), that you completely approve of what your fathers did, because they, on the one hand, killed them and you, on the other hand, build their tombs.

That is why the Wisdom of God said: I will send them prophets and apostles and they will kill and persecute some of them;

That the blood of all the prophets, which has been shed from the foundation of the world, may be required of this generation:

From the blood of Abel to the blood of Zacharias, who was killed between the altar and the temple; yes I am telling you, that it (justice) will be required of this generation.

Shame on you lawyers; you took away the key of knowledge; you did not enter yourselves and you prevented others from entering.

As he went out from there, the scribes and Pharisees began to get very angry and to provoke him to speak on many other things;

Lying in wait for him, to catch him out in something he might say.

Remember, Jesus spoke those words whilst being a guest in the home of a Pharisee; that took real courage!

In Matthew Chapter 21 Verses 12 and 13 we are told that after the triumphal entry into Jerusalem that Jesus went into the temple and caused havoc. He drove out those who were buying and selling and overturned the tables of the moneychangers and upset those who were selling doves and then he publicly accused them of turning the temple of God from a house of prayer into a den of thieves.

David wrote in Psalm 69 Verse 9:
Zeal (fervent desire, righteous indignation) for your house has eaten me up!

The prophet Jeremiah wrote in Chapter 15 Verse 17:
I did not sit among those who were mocking and did not make merry with them. I sat alone because you had your hand upon me, for you have filled me with *indignation!*

Blunt speaking, zeal or righteous indignation when directed by the Holy Spirit can have a place in our lives and in the way we express ourselves, but this must not be confused with anger, irritation or just being 'hot under the collar' about something which we need to keep under proper control.

21. Was not our father Abraham justified by works by offering up his son Isaac on the altar?

22. You can see that faith worked (in conjunction) with his works and by the works, the faith was made perfect;

23. And the scripture was fulfilled which said, 'And Abraham believed God and it was reckoned (counted, considered) to him as righteousness' and he was called the friend of God.

24. You see then that by works a man is justified and not by faith alone.

To our Western minds in the 21st Century most of us struggle with the concept of a father being willing to take the life of his child. We have to remember, therefore, that child sacrifice was not uncommon in the time of Abraham and the test which he put Abraham to was right for the person and the times he lived in.

In Matthew Chapter 10 Verse 37 Jesus said:
Anyone whose love for his father and mother stretches beyond (is greater than) his love for me, is not worthy of me; and anyone whose love for his son or daughter stretches

beyond me (is greater than his love for me), is not worthy of me.

Whilst God will not ask us in the 21st Century to physically take the life of our son or daughter, he still asks us the same questions that he asked of Abraham:
How much do you love me?
Where do your priorities lie?

In answering these two questions we have the opportunity to prove our faith by our actions, but just as the 'angel of the Lord' assisted Abraham, so he will always be there to assist us.

In Romans Chapter 4 Verses 9 to 25 Paul discusses Abraham and the fact that he was justified by faith and points out that he is the father of the circumcised and the uncircumcised, which means that he is the father of every believer and if his faith was credited to him as righteousness by God, then the same rule must apply to us; Praise God!

25. In the same way, was not Rahab the prostitute justified by works, when she entertained the messengers (the spies sent out by Joshua) and sent them on their way by a different route?

The book of Joshua Chapter 2 tells us about the prostitute Rahab who had her home in the actual wall of Jericho. She looked after the two spies that Joshua sent to check out Jericho, she kept them safe and sent them on their way and she lied to the King of Jericho's messenger when he came and asked her about the two spies, in order to protect them.

How on earth can James use this woman, who betrayed her own people, as an example of faith being demonstrated by works, I hear you ask?

I think the answer lies in Chapter 2 Verse 11 where she states:

For the Lord your God, he is the God of heaven above and the earth beneath.

This is a statement of faith, she has no doubts in her heart about the omnipotence of God and his ability to do what he set out to do and she demonstrated that faith by protecting the two spies and sending them on their way and also in believing that God would keep her safe both before and after Jericho was invaded. Let us not forget that if the King of Jericho had found out what she had done that she and most probably her whole family would have been executed.

26. For as the body without the spirit is dead, so also is faith dead without works

Just in case the readers of his letter had not yet got the point, James repeats it just one more time for good measure.

The first training course I remember going on which dealt with the giving of a business presentation had three rules we were expected to follow:
1. Tell them what you are going to tell them (go through the list of topics you intend covering).
2. Tell them (give your detailed presentation).

3. Tell them what you told them (go over the main points very briefly once more).

There was also a fourth un-spoken rule:
If you don't know the answer to a question do not waffle and make sure that you 'Finish on time' and with a final statement of impact.

DISCUSSION SUBJECTS FOR CHAPTER TWO

1. In what situations have you felt discriminated against?

2. Why is 'respect' important in society?

3. Do you think it is important to be punctual? Give your reasons.

4. Jesus said: It is easier for a camel to enter through the eye of a needle, than a rich man to enter into the kingdom of God. Why should this be so?

5. Do we still dishonour the poor?

6. How would you explain 'the royal law' (Verse 8) to a new Christian?

7. Why do you think God made 'You shall not covet' (Exodus Chapter 20 Verse 17) part of the Ten Commandments?

8. In what ways might a Christian relinquish their freedom (Verse 12)?

9. How hard is it to forgive and why is it important for us to do it?

10. How does not using bad language and not telling dirty jokes demonstrate your faith?

11. Why do you think people who believe in God and believe that Jesus actually existed and walked this earth find it difficult to accept him as their Lord and Saviour?

12. In what circumstances might 'righteous indignation' be the correct thing to demonstrate?

13. How might God test a modern day Abraham?

14. How might God use a modern day Rahab?

Chapter Five

COMMENTARY ON THE BOOK OF JAMES

Chapter Three

1. My brothers, (I advise that) not many of you should become teachers, because you know that we (who are teachers) will receive a greater judgement (will be judged more severely).

In John Chapter 3 Verses 1 and 2 we are told:
Now there was a man named Nicodemus, who was a Pharisee and a ruler of the Jews; this man came to him at night and said to him: Rabbi, we know that you are *a teacher* come from God; for no-one can perform the signs that you do, unless God is with him.

In 1 Timothy Chapter 2 Verse 7 Paul said of himself:
I am *a teacher* of the gentiles.
And in 1 Corinthians Chapter 12 Verse 28 Paul lists *teachers* after apostles and prophets in his list of the offices that God has appointed to his church.

This warning from James is not stated anywhere else in the New Testament but apart from Jesus and Paul I could not find anyone else in the early church who claimed to be a teacher, so it would be safe to presume that it was a very highly esteemed office and James was anxious to remind people of that fact and that they should not appoint anyone to this position who was not worthy of it and for no-one to allow themselves to be appointed as a teacher without understanding the high office and responsibility that they were taking on.

How remiss we are therefore, when we appoint new converts with little training and no supervision to be our Sunday School teachers, teaching the most vulnerable members of our church. I count myself fortunate that the church I attended when young had a dedicated band of experienced older men and women who took on the task of teaching the children the truths of the gospel.

From observing my own children as they went through their school years, it was obvious that the better teachers achieved far more than those who were just in it for the money or the convenience of the hours.

The warning - *will receive a greater judgement (will be judged more severely)* should be taken very seriously by anyone who aspires to be a teacher in God's church and they should think very carefully about every word and phrase they use when they are teaching members of the flock. Careless examples or inappropriate references can cause a lot of damage that we teachers will be accountable for.

2. For in many respects we all stumble (we all make mistakes); but if someone does not stumble with regard to the things he says, then that person is a perfect man and is able to bridle (control) his whole body.

James affirms that we all make mistakes and get things wrong from time to time, that is only to be expected and we can seek forgiveness from God and get ourselves right with him again when we realise our error. If however, we make serious mistakes in what we say to people, especially when in a 'teaching' role, where we are considered to be a person of knowledge and influence, then those words might permanently damage or mislead someone else, a much more serious matter which is why he stresses the importance of 'not stumbling' with regard to the things we say.

Being able to 'bridle' or have complete control of our tongue is important, whatever our role might be in life, but for a teacher it is an absolutely essential quality and no-one should be appointed to that role who does not possess that quality.

It is better to leave the role of teacher un-filled, than to appoint the wrong person!

3. Behold, we put bits into the mouths of horses in order to make them obey us and (through those bits) we can direct their whole bodies.

4. Consider also ships, which though they are so great and are driven along by strong winds yet are steered by a very little helm (rudder) wherever the person steering it should decide to go.

5. Even so, the tongue is also a small member but is capable of being very boastful. Just think of how a small fire can burn down a great wood!

Every week we here about someone who has harmed themselves or even taken their own life because of what someone has said either to their face or behind their back or through Social Media.

We read of young impressionable men and women who abandon their country and parents and friends after being radicalised by someone they don't know and who possibly lives in another country.

Never before have we needed to be so diligent in regard to what we say and write and 'post' on Social Media and what we listen to and read for ourselves.

There is a computer expression that I picked up very early on in my career as a systems analyst and that is 'Garbage In – Garbage Out' or GIGO for short. No matter how brilliant the computer system might be, if the data you put into it is rubbish, then the output can only be rubbish as well.

Proverbs Chapter 17 Verse 28 informs us that:
Even a fool can appear to be wise when he keeps silent and is considered to be perceptive when he keeps his mouth shut.

In Verse 5 James talks about the damage a small fire can cause and last year I witnessed firsthand the devastation caused by a single lightening strike that started a forest fire.

It burned for days and took several lives as well as destroying dozens of homes and hundreds of acres of crops and forests. That is how damaging James considered our tongues to be when we do not have proper control over them.

James also mentions that our tongues are *'capable of being very boastful'* something which he obviously disapproved of; but what is wrong with 'blowing your own trumpet' as we 'Brits' might say?

I think that this is one of those difficult subjects where different cultures can hold differing views about boasting.

I remember as a child being told at someone's birthday party, just after the jelly and ice-cream had been placed on the table:

Those who ask don't get and those who don't ask, don't want.

To which I replied:

If I am not allowed to ask but lose out if I don't, what am I supposed to do?

The answer came back:

You must wait until you are asked first and then you can reply.

A similar response might be given in relation to boasting. There is nothing wrong with stating your qualifications, experience, personal attributes etc. in relation to a direct question, but you should not use the occasion to exaggerate your abilities or as a way of putting someone else down.

1 Kings Chapter 20 Verse 11 tells of a reply which King Ahab, King of Israel gave to Ben-Hadad, King of Syria:

The person who is in the act of putting his armour on (who is about to go out to battle), should not be boasting like the person who is in the process of taking it off (after he has come home from defeating his enemy).

David wrote in Psalm 34 Verses 1 to 3:
I will bless the Lord at all times: his praise will continually be in my mouth.

My soul shall make its *boast* in the Lord (My whole being is proud to belong to the Lord): the humble will hear about it and be glad.

Come and join me in glorifying the Lord and let us lift on high his name together.

As Christians we should be like David and be proud, even boastful of all that Jesus had done for the world at large and for us in particular.

On a practical note, during my time as a Personnel Manager (H.R. Manager) I carried out many interviews and was always switched off by an applicant who had made claims about their qualifications or experience in their C.V. which were obviously false or overstated and was always impressed when someone's C.V. was shown to be accurate or even slightly under-stated.

6. And the tongue is a fire, acting as a world of iniquity; as it sits among the members of our bodies, staining the whole body and inflaming the course of nature (setting the direction of a person's life on fire) and it is set on fire itself, by hell.

Just as a small fire can end up by burning down a great forest, so the tongue, (a small muscle attached to the floor of our mouths) or more precisely the words it utters, can stain or even destroy our whole body, nature or future.

As a young man I was told:
If you cannot say something nice about a person, then do not say anything at all.
Once your thoughts have been vocalized, you cannot take them back. You may regret them; you may be truly penitent; but the damage has been done and the person you said them to will always wonder if you really meant what you said or not.

Evil or hurtful words do not come from any heavenly source; they come from the devil, which is why James concludes Verse 6 by saying: *and it* (the tongue or the bad words it utters) *is set on fire itself, by hell.*

7. For every kind of beast, whether birds, or reptiles or marine creatures is tamed and has been tamed by man;

8. But no man is able to tame the tongue; it is an unruly evil, full of deadly poison.

In the two thousand or so years since James wrote those words and in particular, in the last one hundred and fifty years, man has achieved some amazing things. Radio, television, communications, transport, space travel, manufacture, medicine, the list is endless, yet with all this progress, we seem to have more strife and more worldly problems than ever before, much of which started with an ill conceived comment or a statement which should not have been made.

Man is just as incapable today in controlling his tongue as he was in James' time, but with modern communications and an ever active world-wide media, we must all be on our guard not to make the situation worse and with the World-Wide-Web we can be pretty certain that whatever we do say, will be recorded, will be available to everyone with access to the Internet and will probably be around until the end of the world comes.

9. By this tongue we bless the Lord and Father and by the same tongue we curse our fellow man who has been created in the likeness of God:

10. So that out of the same mouth comes forth both blessing and cursing. My brothers, these things ought not to be.

11. Can a fountain (or spring) send out both sweet and bitter water from the same hole?

12. My brothers, can a fig tree produce olives or a vine produce figs? Neither can a salt water fountain (or spring) make sweet water.

Hypocrisy is the practice of professing views, beliefs or standards which are in fact contrary to a person's character or behaviour, especially in relation to piety or virtue.

A Hypocrite is someone who pretends to be one thing when he is in fact something else.

One of the reasons I have often heard quoted as to why someone would not want to attend a church goes something like this:

'I would not dream of joining that bunch of hypocrites. You should hear their language and see what they get up to when they are away from their church. I may not be perfect but at least I do not pretend to be something I am not.'

The child abuse scandals which have rocked so many of our denominations over the past twenty years have done incalculable harm to God's church and we, if only by association, have been tarnished by these scandals as well, which is why our language and behaviour have to be exemplary in order to start to build confidence once again in the Christian church.

The examples James gives of a fig tree and a fountain do not need any explanation and certainly stand the test of time, being as true today as they were when he wrote them, therefore, let us be on our guard so that we do not praise God with one breath and curse our fellow man with the next.

13A. Who among you is wise and has understanding?

It is easy to assume that the question at the start of this verse is a 'rhetorical' question, i.e. a question posed for effect when the asker of the question is not expecting a reply, but I am not sure that this assumption would be correct because it requires each of us to give a truthful answer, before we go on to the second half of the verse.

Remember that James talked about wisdom in Chapter 1 Verse 5 so he is making sure that we have all asked God for wisdom and that we are now ready to discuss the responsibilities which this wisdom lays upon us.

If, in being honest with ourselves, we should reply that we are not wise and do not have understanding, then like a 'loop' in a computer program, we need to go back to Chapter 1 Verse 5 and start again, because the Christian life is a progression and we need to have assimilated the basics before we can get on with the more complex matters.

In 1 Corinthians Chapter 3 Verse 2 Paul berates the members of the church at Corinth because they refused to become mature Christians, he said to them:

I fed you with milk and not solid food because up to now that was all you were able to accept and even now you are still not able to take anything other than milk!

Hebrews Chapter 5 Verse 12 to Chapter 6 Verse 2 also talks of the need for believers to become spiritually mature.

At the end of his ministry, just before he went up into heaven, Jesus left this last instruction with his disciples in Matthew Chapter 28 Verses 18 to 20:

And Jesus approached them and began to talk with them, saying: All authority in heaven and on the earth was given to me.

Go, therefore, *making disciples of all the nations*, baptizing them in the name of the Father and of the Son and of the Holy Spirit;

Teaching them to observe absolutely everything that I gave commands to you about; and behold, I am with you every single day, right up to the completion of the age.

If we are a true disciple then we are progressing in our faith as Jesus requested, so we can now consider the responsibilities that come with being wise and understanding.

13B. Let him show it by his good conduct, by his works which are carried out in the humility which comes from wisdom.

James talks about a believer having 'good conduct' and Paul touches on this when he wrote to his young friend in 1 Timothy Chapter 4 Verse 12, when he said:

Do not let anyone despise your youth but be an example to the believers in word (what you say and in what you preach), in conduct, in love, in faith, in spirit and in purity.

In other words, do not let them find anything in any aspect of your life that they can criticise or complain to me about.

We read in John Chapter 13 Verse 15, after Jesus had washed the feet of his disciples that he said to them:

For I have given you an example, that you should also do, as I have done to you.

That is the level of 'good conduct' that James was speaking about, so it is interesting that he mentions that the works we perform should be carried out in the *'humility which comes from wisdom.'*

In Verse 5 James talked about not being boastful in what we had to say about ourselves and here he talks about being humble when we carry out our 'good conduct' works.

This is not to say that there is anything wrong in feeling good about the things we do for the Lord, it would be strange if we did not, but if we have the *wisdom of God*, then we will know how to behave and what our disposition should be so that the recipient of our 'good works' does not feel put down or obligated towards us but recognizes that the love of Christ has been at work through us.

14. But if you have bitter jealousy and rivalry in your hearts, do not be jubilant about it and lie against (deny) the truth.

15. This wisdom has not come down from above, but is earthly, sensual, of the devil.

16. For where jealousy and rivalry are, there is tumult (uproar, confusion, disturbance) and every evil practice.

What! Jealousy and rivalry in the church!! Surely not, I hear you say, but alas, it was there in the early church and it still exists today in its many guises.

Paul touched on this subject in 1 Corinthians Chapter 1 Verses 12 and 13 when he reprimanded the Corinthians for claiming to follow this teacher in preference to that teacher or being baptised by this person rather than that person, but as Paul pointed out we should all be followers of Jesus and not put others down by claiming allegiances or knowledge that others might not be party to.

We all know how infuriating it is when a person claims to have certain knowledge about someone or something but then informs us that they cannot divulge this knowledge or the source of this knowledge because it is a secret or they have promised to keep a confidence.

Even with Jesus' own disciples there were problems. In Mark Chapter 10 Verses 35 to 45 we read of how the two brothers, James and John went to Jesus and asked a favour of him, that they might sit, one on his left hand and one on his right, in glory. Jesus dealt firmly with this request but we read in verse 41 that the other disciples started to become very displeased with James and John; rivalry can happen through the simplest and most unimportant of issues.

For example:

Who is asked to read the bible and pray in church and who is always ignored, except when it comes to doing the most mundane of tasks?

Who always has to play second fiddle because the person doing the top job has done it for the last twenty five years and does not wish to relinquish it?

Who always wears new clothes and whose are patched and hand-me-downs?

Who gets all the admiring glances and pleasant comments and who goes unnoticed?

Jealousy and rivalry and the malicious thoughts and comments that can accompany them are most definitely not from God, as James states in Verse 15:

This wisdom has not come down from above, but is earthly, sensual, of the devil

and needs to be dealt with swiftly and firmly before:

'uproar, confusion, disturbance and every evil practice'

tears the church apart.

17. But the wisdom which is from above is first of all pure, then peaceable (quiet, tranquil, peaceful, not at war), self-controlled, submissive, full of mercy and good fruits, without partiality and hypocrisy.

What a contrast between God's wisdom and the devil's wisdom.

God's Wisdom is pure.

Free from taint or pollution, clean and wholesome.

Hebrews Chapter 4 Verse 12 says:

The word of God is alive and powerful and sharper than any two-edged sword, piercing and dividing soul and spirit and joints and marrow as well as being able to discern (read or discover) the very thoughts and intentions of the heart.

When we have wisdom from God it can have a similar effect to the 'word of God' because they both come from the same source.

I recall the first Youth Camp we helped to organise in 1976 and the awful shock we had when we discovered a week or so before the event that the tents we had ordered for the young people were not available. The leaders met together and prayed about the situation and then someone had a great idea which we all accepted and acted upon and by the time the date to start the camp had arrived, so had all the tents we needed.

I have absolutely no doubt that the wisdom we received at that meeting came from God, because the solution seemed so simple and obvious and we all agreed to it without hesitation and it worked out perfectly.

It is peaceable
Quiet, tranquil, calm, peaceful, not at war.

In John Chapter 14 Verse 27 Jesus said:
Peace I leave to you, my peace I give to you; not as the world gives, do I give to you. Do not let your heart be troubled, neither let it be fearful.

As Christians we should expect to enjoy the 'peace of God' because Jesus said he would give it to us and he never lied, so if you are not enjoying this peace, no matter what your situation, then the devil is cheating you out of it and you need to tell him to go and to ask Jesus for a fresh infilling of his peace and of his wisdom to help and guide you through your current situation.

When we all arrived at the meeting to discuss the missing tents, we were anything but peaceable, but in a very short period of time the peace of God descended upon each one of us and we just knew that God would show us a way through this problem. The peace we experienced that day was so real that you felt you could almost reach out and touch it.

It is Self-controlled

We have already talked a lot about self-control in the previous notes but again it shows how important this 'Fruit of the Spirit' is for Christians that James should mention it yet again.

It is Submissive

The state of being in submission, being humble.

The writer to the Hebrews stated in Chapter 13 Verse 17:
You should obey those who rule over you (spiritually speaking) and be submissive, for they watch out for your souls.

Being submissive does not mean that we should let someone else walk all over us and run our life for us. Each one of us will be accountable for the decisions we have made and the things that we have said and done and it will not be of any use to point our finger at someone else and say, 'They told me to do it.'

If the heavenly knowledge we have been given affects our church or fellowship, then naturally we should share it with those in charge, but we should do this quietly and reverently, without trying to undermine their authority or confidence.

Where the knowledge only concerns ourselves, or those close to us, then we need to submit to the guidance of the Holy Spirit in how we deal with this knowledge and how we explain it to the ones we love and are responsible for.

I remember being very concerned about telling my wife that I thought we should move house and go and live and work in a town we had never visited and where we did not know anyone who lived there. I prayed about the matter and asked the Holy Spirit for guidance as to how I should explain this to her and in the end we both agreed it was the right move for us and the family, as time has proved it to be.

It is Full of Mercy
To be compassionate and forgiving towards someone who has offended us or thinks of us as an adversary.

James talked about Mercy in relation to forgiveness in Chapter 2 Verse 13 but there is another form of 'intellectual' mercy, where we let someone 'off the hook' about something, where we know they are wrong in what they have said or at fault in what they have done, in order to save them from humiliation.

It is Full of Good Fruits
In Luke Chapter 3 Verses 7 to 9 we read of John the Baptist:
He said, therefore, to the crowds who were going out to be baptised by him: Children of vipers, who has warned you to flee from the coming wrath?

Produce, therefore, fruits that are worthy of repentance and do not begin to say among yourselves: Abraham is our father; for I am telling you that God can raise up children to Abraham out of these stones.

Even as I speak, the axe has already been laid at the root of the trees; every tree, therefore, not producing *good fruit* is being cut down and is being thrown into the fire.

Jesus stated in Matthew Chapter 7 Verse 17:

Every good tree bears *good fruit* and every bad tree bears bad fruit.

And concludes the discourse in Verse 20 by saying:

Therefore, you will know them 'by their fruits'.

If the wisdom you received bears 'good fruit' it was from God but if the wisdom you received bears 'bad fruit' it is not from God.

How easy a test is that?

It is Without Partiality

Without prejudice, fair, un-biased.

We all like to think of ourselves as being 'impartial' but it is so hard to achieve. What we grew up with is often what we consider to be normal, but it could be entirely different from what someone else might consider to be normal.

I grew up in London with a whole range of shops within five minutes of where I lived and four cinemas and a department store and a railway station within fifteen minutes of where I lived. To me, that was normal; so to go and live somewhere where just a fraction of these amenities was a twenty minute drive away was not normal and I was prejudiced against living in such a place.

With regard to my church life, I grew up with the King James Bible, with the wonderful old hymns of Wesley and the like and where the men of the church were in charge of things and I have struggled sometimes to be fair minded and un-biased about some of the changes that the church has seen over the last sixty years.

Imagine the shock-waves and outrage Jesus must have caused when he performed his miracles on the Sabbath, or when he actually touched the sick and diseased and when he allowed a woman of ill repute to anoint his feet with expensive perfume, not to mention when he upset the tables in the temple.

If the wisdom we get is not un-biased and impartial, we should question its source.

It is Without Hypocrisy

Hypocrisy was discussed earlier in this Chapter.

18. When peacemakers sow in peace there is a harvest of righteousness.

This verse stands in stark contrast to Verse 16 which talks of uproar, confusion, disturbance and evil practices.

It reminds me of the sower Jesus talked about in Luke Chapter 8 Verses 4 to 8 going out into his field with his bag of seed on a beautiful calm Spring day and just throwing the seed all around him and then coming back a few weeks later to see the new shoots coming through the ground.

When we are filled with the peace of God and are fulfilling the role of 'peacemaker' rather than 'troublemaker' we too can produce a harvest of righteousness from the fields where we have sown and like the sower, we too should be able to see new shoots that were not there before we arrived on the scene.

Notice how definite James is in Verse 18. He doesn't say that they might or could produce a harvest he says that 'there is a harvest' which will come from our sowing the seed.

Just as the word of God which goes forth from His mouth, does not return to Him void (Isaiah Chapter 55 Verse 11) so the wisdom of God which we speak or demonstrate has a lasting effect even if we are not around to gather in the harvest.

Earlier in the Chapter when talking about 'God's Wisdom is Pure' (Verse 17) I mentioned a Youth Camp I was involved with in 1976. Well, throughout the week of the camp we had one problem after another to overcome and by the Friday night many of us were exhausted and were ready to go home when suddenly the peace of God fell over the whole camp and the Holy Spirit moved through the camp.

Within a very short space of time the leaders, who had gathered together to chat, started to get reports of things happening in the camp and that evening somewhere in the region of sixteen young people gave their hearts to the Lord.

I personally had the privilege of leading several of them to the Lord and since I had only been working with them for a few months I was amazed that this transformation had happened so quickly until I felt the Holy Spirit say to me that I was but the reaper of this particular harvest, others had faithfully sown into the lives of these young people over a much longer period of time.

Lets us not forget to ask God to enable us to be his peacemakers that we too may sow in peace and produce a harvest of righteousness.

DISCUSSION SUBJECTS FOR CHAPTER THREE

1. What is the role of teachers in society?

2. Why are there so many angry people around?

3. Define a gossip!

4. What sort of good fruit would you like to produce?

5. Why can arrogance and pride be so damaging in a church fellowship?

6. Where, other than in your church fellowship, have you encountered jealousy and rivalry and what effect did it have?

7. What is the difference between being 'submissive' and being 'subservient'?

8. What form might a 'harvest of righteousness' take?

Chapter Six

COMMENTARY ON THE BOOK OF JAMES

Chapter Four

1A. From where do wars and fighting among you come?

Mankind has been asking this same question for millennia.

Why do we constantly have wars and fighting somewhere in the world?

Why can't people get on with each other?

Why is the arms trade so huge and why is such a large percentage of most countries GDP spent on weapons and defence?

Do you remember when the Berlin wall came down and the 'Cold War' supposedly came to an end and politicians talked about a 'Peace Dividend'? Well where is it?

The early church must have had a lot of disputes and infighting going on for James to open the chapter with such a statement as this. This first verse suggests that they had real problems in the early church which he was not prepared to brush under the carpet but wanted to bring them out into the open and to deal with them head on.

Any fellowship which is incapable of dealing with its differences and problems in a loving, Christ-like way will eventually tear itself apart and die.

Having asked the question, the second half of the verse provides the answer,

1B. Do they not come as a result of the desires which are battling within you?

Man's desires to conquer, to kill, to remove anyone with an opposing ideology or way of life, to take from someone else something which they have decided that they want or need, or simply to show that they are bigger and better and more powerful than the next man, tribe or people are wrong in the sight of God and these wrong desires lead to wars and fighting.

If we have the wisdom which comes from God (Chapter 1 Verse 5) then like Paul we should all be able to claim that we have the mind of Christ (1 Corinthians Chapter 2 Verse 16) in which case there would always be agreement within the church, because Christ is not divided, he cannot disagree with himself.

How sad Jesus must be to see the way that his church has split into different factions and then split again and again, with some branches of his church being openly hostile towards others and some even considering themselves superior to others.

I remember being in a fellowship where I felt hostility towards several other people in the same fellowship. I knew my hostility was wrong and prayed that Jesus would change the way I felt about them but in the meantime that he would give me his love for these individuals.

Over the next year or so I came to see these people in an entirely new light and instead of noticing the things about them which irritated me, I started to notice how much they loved their Lord and how much work they did for him. Within a short period of time I had completely changed my opinion of these people and felt a genuine love for them and an appreciation for all they did in the church.

I urge you, therefore, if you know that you have negative feelings about someone in your fellowship, that you ask Jesus to change the way you think about them, but in case that takes a while, to ask him to replace your negative thoughts with his love for them in the meantime.

2. You desire and don't have (what you desire); you murder and are jealous and are not able to obtain (what you want); you fight and you war. You do not have because you do not ask.

In Chapter 1 Verses 14 and 15 we looked at 'wrongful desires' and James picks up the subject again in Verse 2 and the next few verses but the new thought presented by James here is :

You do not have because you do not ask.

Matthew Chapter 7 Verses 7 and 8 quotes Jesus as saying:

Ask (and keep on asking), and it shall be given to you; seek (and keep on seeking), and you shall find; knock (and keep on knocking), and it shall be opened to you.

For everyone who asks, receives; and the one who is seeking, finds; and to the one who is knocking, it shall be opened.

Matthew Chapter 21 Verses 22 quotes Jesus as saying:

And everything that you ask for in prayer, if you believe, you will receive.

Luke Chapter 11 Verses 9 and 10 quotes Jesus as saying:

And I tell you, ask (and keep on asking) and it will be given to you, seek (and keep on seeking) and you will find, knock (and keep on knocking) and it will be opened to you.

For everyone who is asking, receives and anyone who is seeking, finds and anyone who is knocking, will have it opened.

John Chapter 14 Verses 12 to 14 quotes Jesus as saying to his disciples:

Truly, truly I tell you, that the one who believes in me, will also do the same works which I do and greater works than these will he do, because I am going to the Father;

And whatever you ask in my name, this I will do, that the Father may be glorified in the Son.

If you ask me for anything in my name, I will do it.

Jesus said quite clearly that if we ask then we will receive but most of us would have to admit that we have not always got what we asked for, but that should not stop us from asking.

Whilst I do not believe that my prayers can extend my time on this earth for a single second past what is written in the Lamb's Book of Life and neither would I want them to, I do believe that my prayers can have a considerable effect on the quality of life that both I and my loved ones can enjoy.

This means that I regularly mention our health, our safety, our diet, our peace of mind and a lot of other personal matters in my prayers. I take Jesus at his word and ask for all sorts of things and although I think it would be cheating to ask him for victory when I am playing bowls, I do ask him to help me to play to the best of my ability.

So if we have been given the 'green light' to ask God for things, why don't we always get what we ask for?

3. When you ask, you do not receive, as you are asking for the wrong things; because you want them to indulge your own pleasures.

According to James, we do not receive what we have been asking for because we have been asking for the wrong things.

If the two year-old child you were looking after asked you for a box of matches to play with you would say no. The child could set light to themselves or they might burn the house down.

If a ten year-old asked for the keys of your car in order to take his friends for a drive to the shops, again, for obvious reasons, you would say no.

As responsible adults, we would not give inappropriate gifts to children and sometimes, the things we ask God for are not appropriate for us, so we don't get them.

In Luke Chapter 18 Verses 1 to 8 Jesus told a parable about a certain poor widow:

There was a certain judge in a certain city, who did not fear God or have any regard for man. And there was a widow in that city and she came to him saying: Give me justice from my opponent.

And for a time he would not; but after a while he said to himself: Although I do not fear God or have regard for man, yet, because this widow is causing me a lot of trouble, I will give her justice, unless she should exhaust me with her continual coming.

And the Lord said: Listen to what the unrighteous judge says; and will God, by no means (at least do the same and) give justice to his chosen ones, who cry out to him day and night and will he not have patience with them?

I tell you that he will give them justice speedily. Nevertheless, will the Son of man find faith on the earth when he comes?

Jesus is telling us that we should be persistent in our prayers and entreaties and that God does not give us everything we ask for, at the first time of asking, but his comment in the last verse suggests that we need to have 'faith' for the things we are asking him for.

In the quotation from Matthew Chapter 21 Verse 22, Jesus said:
And everything that you ask for *in prayer,* if you *believe,* you will receive.

Prayer is us talking to God and him talking to us. We are coming into the presence of the creator of heaven and earth so we need to be respectful, polite and to think about what we are saying and what we are asking for and that the thing we are asking for would not offend him or contravene his holy law.

Jesus also mentions 'belief' or faith in God's ability to grant us our prayer.

In the quotations from John Chapter 14 verses 12 to 14 it certainly ends with the statement:
If you ask me for anything in my name, I will do it.

But the previous verses talk about discipleship and doing the works he did. If you don't give Jesus a thought or walk in his ways until you want something, it can come as no surprise if he does not always give you what you have asked for.

James ends Verse 3 by saying:

because you want them (the things you have been asking for) to indulge your own pleasures.

I don't believe James is saying that having some pleasures in your life is wrong, but I think what he is saying here is, if that is all you are living for, selfish ambition, status, wealth and worldly pleasures then you are in error and don't expect God to answer your prayers in the way you want him to.

Although not quite in the same vein I remember once asking God to give me patience, as I recognised that I was quite low on it at the time (and others did occasionally hint at the same thing to me).
Unfortunately for me, I had not realised that patience was not a gift of the spirit but a fruit of the spirit, so it was not something that God could just zap me with and I would have it. Instead, for the next couple of years he put me to work with three of the most difficult people that I ever came across in my whole working life, but by the end of that time, I was a much more patient person than I had been at the beginning.

We really do have to scrutinize our motives when we ask God for things to make sure that we are not just indulging our earthly pleasures.

A final point to make is that we can, for the best of motives, be asking for the wrong thing, particularly when praying for others and doing what Jesus told us to do in John Chapter 14 Verse 12:
The one who believes in me, will also do the same works which I do.

We read in Matthew Chapter 4 Verse 24 that:
And they brought to Jesus all the sick people who had various diseases and other problems as well as those who were possessed by demons along with epileptics and paralytics AND HE HEALED THEM.

When Jesus sent seventy two of his disciples out into the villages as recorded in Luke Chapter 10, he told them in verse 9 to:
Heal the sick that are there and tell them: The kingdom of God has drawn near to you.

So quite clearly, as his modern day disciples, he expects us to follow in his footsteps and to heal the sick. Now few of us will be called upon to hold mass rallies where thousands of sick people come to be healed, but we will regularly find ourselves on a one to one basis with someone who is sick or needy and needs prayer.

No need to panic, because in I Corinthians Chapter 12 verses 1 to 11 Paul talks about the 'Gifts of the Spirit' and there are many excellent books which talk in detail about the 'Gifts' but I would like to point out that Verse 9 mentions the Gift of Healing along with the Gift of Faith and the previous verse talks about the Gifts of Wisdom and Knowledge and the following verse talks about the Gift of Discernment.
In my opinion, to pray for the sick and needy, we should ask God for all five of these gifts.
We need the gift of Faith for ourselves and the one we are praying for, so that we might not have any doubts.

We need the gift of Discernment to be able to tell if the person we are about to pray for is under demonic attack.

We need the Gift of Knowledge to know what is wrong and what we need to be praying for.

We need the Gift of Wisdom to know what to say and how to say it and lastly we need the Gift of Healing so that the person might be made well again.

Asking for the right thing, with the right motives, is so important if we are to fulfil our role as disciples.

4. You adulterers and adulteresses, don't you know that friendship with the world is enmity (hostility, hatred, animosity) towards God? Whoever therefore, resolves to be a friend of the world is establishing themselves as an enemy of God.

James is talking here about where our loyalties and priorities lie and that we cannot compromise with the world when it comes to our faith, our behaviour and God's law.

By picking out adulterers and adulteresses he is addressing the immorality which was present in many parts of the early church as it is today.

In 1 Corinthians Chapter 5 Paul warns the church in Corinth of the need to deal quite firmly with anyone in the fellowship who is living an immoral life.

Paul warns the Galatians in Chapter 5 Verses 1 to 7 about avoiding fornication (sexual immorality) and uncleanness and in Colossians Chapter 3 Verse 5 they too are warned about the evils of fornication.

Before we tick this verse off as not applying to us, let us not forget what Jesus said in Matthew Chapter 5 Verses 27 and 28:

You have heard that it was said to those of old that they should not commit adultery, but I am telling you that whoever looks at a woman/man in a lustful way has already committed adultery with her/him in his/her heart.

I would suggest that Jesus' comments on the subject should be taken very seriously and since he does not specify that the person you are looking lustfully at has to be standing in front of you then it could be a drawing, a painting, a photograph or a video clip of them.

In the 21st Century we are constantly surrounded by pictures, videos and other representations of beautiful people that are trying to persuade us to buy whatever it is they are selling, including themselves sometimes.

Temptation is always close at hand which is why the Lord's Prayer closes with the lines:

And lead us **not** into temptation; but **deliver** us from evil:

For thine (yours) is the kingdom, the **power** and the glory; for ever and ever.

Amen

We can only resist temptation with God's help, for we are all weak and the devil knows what our weaknesses are but God is all powerful and with his help we can walk that fine line of being 'in' the world but not 'of' the world and remaining God's friend rather than the world's friend.

5. Or do you think that the scripture says for no reason that 'The Spirit which dwells in you enviously desires (after worldly pleasures)'.

To enviously desire something we do not have is to covet it and while we do not know which specific scripture James was referring to here we do know that the tenth commandment says:
You shall not covet (strongly desire) your neighbour's house, **you shall not covet your neighbour's wife,** nor his male and female servants, nor his ox, nor his ass, nor any other thing that is your neighbour's.

Much of the book of Proverbs warns of the dangers of sexual immorality, Chapter 7 in particular warns that we should avoid this particular temptation as it is the pathway to hell (Verse 27).
James knows that it is mans natural instinct to seek that which is 'forbidden fruit' as demonstrated by Adam and Eve in the Garden of Eden which is why so much of God's law deals with what we are not allowed to do which is why it is so liberating that this whole law of negative commands can be summed up positively by the following short statement:
You should love the Lord your God with all your heart and with all your soul and with all your strength and with all your mind and your neighbour as yourself.

6. But the grace he gives us is even greater; for which reason scripture says, 'God resists those who are arrogant but he gives grace to those who are humble'.

No matter what the temptation God's grace is more than sufficient to enable us to resist it and to overcome it and put it behind us and move on with our Christian walk, but no matter what the temptation or addiction may be, we first have to recognise that we have a problem and then we need to humble ourselves and ask for God's forgiveness and for his help.

There is no place in God's church for the arrogant.
He said through Isaiah the prophet, Chapter 13 Verse 11:
I will cause the arrogance of the proud to cease and I will lay low the haughtiness of the terrible.

Jesus firmly quashed the idea of leaders or anyone else in his church being proud or arrogant when he said in Matthew Chapter 20 Verse 27:
Whoever desires to be chief among you, let him be your servant.

To receive the 'Grace of God' we need to have a humble and contrite (remorseful) heart for it tells us in Psalm 51 Verse 17:
The sacrifices of God are a broken spirit, a broken and contrite heart O God, you will not despise.

7. Submit yourselves therefore, to God; but oppose the devil and he will flee from you.

In Luke Chapter 22 Verses 41 to 43 we read:
And withdrawing a stone's throw away from them, he (Jesus) kneeled and prayed, saying:

Father, if you are willing, remove this cup from me: nevertheless, not my will, but yours, be done.

And an angel from heaven appeared to him, strengthening him.

Immediately after that act of submission by Jesus to his Father's will, an angel was dispatched to strengthen him, that is how quickly God can answer our prayers when we humble ourselves and submit to his will.

Like Jesus the 'cup', problem, persecution, sickness, whatever it might be will not always be removed, but like him we can expect to be strengthened so that we can endure it.

Just as Jesus gave us an example of submission he also showed us how to 'oppose the devil'. In Mark Chapter 8 Verse 33 it tells us that after Peter had taken Jesus aside and rebuked him that Jesus then rebuked Peter by saying:

Get thee behind me Satan.

The devil can take many guises and may even speak to you through people you know but when the gift of discernment is operating in your life (and you only have to ask for it) the Holy Spirit who dwells in you will give you a warning and whether you say it out loud or quietly to yourself, you should copy what Jesus said i.e. I am a child of God so you just get behind me Satan.

8. Draw near to God and he will draw near to you. Cleanse your hands you sinners and purify your hearts you double minded (hypocrites).

Jesus said in Matthew Chapter 11 Verse 28:

Come (draw near) to me all you who are weary and are heavily laden (with worldly cares, troubles and sins) and I will give you rest (draw near to you).

Again he invites us to draw near to him in John Chapter 6 Verse 35:

Jesus said to them: I am the bread of life, the one who comes (draws near) to me shall not be hungry again and the one who believes on me, will never thirst again.

In John Chapter 5 Verses 39 and 40 Jesus said to the Jews who had been berating him:

You search the scriptures because you think they contain the way to eternal life and it is these very scriptures which testify about me, but you are not willing to come (draw near) to me in order that you might have eternal life.

There is no ambiguity in what James is saying in this verse, if we do not choose to draw near to God then he will not force himself upon us and he will not draw near to us, which means that we cannot feed on the 'bread of life' and we cannot enjoy eternal life with Jesus.

I wonder if James had Psalm 24 Verses 3 and 4 in mind when he wrote those words because David wrote:

Who may ascend the hill of the Lord (draw near to God) or who may stand in his holy place (in his presence)?

He (everyone) who has clean hands and a pure heart, who has not lifted up his soul to an idol (practiced idolatry) or sworn deceitfully (lied or given false witness).

Once again James mentions the sin of hypocrisy which we looked at in Chapter 3 verses 9 to 12.

In John Chapter 15 Verses 1 to 5 Jesus told us how we might be clean and stay effective for him:

I am the true vine and my Father is the gardener. Every branch in me that does not bear fruit, he takes it away and every branch that bears fruit he prunes, so that it will bear more fruit.

Now *you are clean* because of the word which I have spoken to you; remain in me and I will remain you.

As the branch cannot bear fruit of itself, unless it remains in the vine, so you cannot either, unless you remain in me.

I am the vine and you are the branches. The one who *remains in me and I in him,* the same brings forth much fruit, for without me you can do nothing.

9. Be distressed and mourn and weep; let your laughter be turned to mourning and your joy to dejection (heaviness, depression).

10. Humble yourselves before the Lord and he will exalt you (raise you up).

There is a big difference between being truly sorry for something we have done which we honestly regret and being sorry that someone caught us doing something we should not have done.

Anyone who has ever had anything to do with children will know how quickly a naughty child will apologize when caught out doing something they have been told not to do, especially if there is likely to be any sort of punishment and how often they will do the same thing again when they think no-one is looking.

In Jonah Chapter 3 Verse 6 to 9 we are told that the king of Nineveh took off his royal robes and put on sackcloth and sat in ashes on hearing the word which Jonah was proclaiming that Nineveh would be destroyed in forty days. He also issued a royal decree that the citizens of Nineveh should do the same and that everyone should join him in a fast and should turn from their evil ways.

As a result of their actions we read in Chapter 3 Verse 10 that God saw what they were doing and relented from what he had planned for them.

Jesus paid a terrible price so that we might receive forgiveness of our sins but that does not mean that we should go on sinning just because the price has already been paid.

When we become aware of sin in our lives we should be truly penitent and humble ourselves before God and tearfully seek his forgiveness and cleansing, because there can be no forgiveness when we are not sincerely sorry for what we have done wrong, but just sorry that God (or man) found out about it

11. Do not speak against one another brothers. Whoever speaks against his brother or judges his brother speaks against the law and judges the law, and if you judge the law you are not a doer of the law but a judge (of the law).

12. There is one lawgiver and judge who is able to save and to destroy; so who are you to judge your neighbour?

Backbite – to talk spitefully about someone.

According to my 'Cruden's Complete Concordance' the words 'backbiters, backbiteth (backbite) and backbiting' only appear four times in the bible.

Romans Chapter 1 Verse 30: Where Paul lists backbiters among the list of those who hate God.

Psalm 15 Verse 3: Where David lists those who do not backbite as being among those who may dwell in his sanctuary and live on his holy hill.

Proverbs 25 Verse 23 warns:

As the north wind brings rain, so a backbiting tongue causes an angry countenance.

2Corinthians Chapter 12 Verse 20. In writing to the church at Corinth Paul says to them:

For I am fearful that when I come to visit you next that you will not be what I am hoping to find and that I will not be what you are hoping to find because I might discover that you are contentious, jealous, unruly, selfish, backbiting, whispering (gossips), conceited and disorderly.

Gossip – casual, idle chatter which could be malicious and rumour spreading.

Paul mentions gossips in his list above as being something he does not want to find in the church.

Proverbs Chapter 16 Verse 28 warns:

A gossip can separate the best of friends.

And proverbs Chapter 26 Verse 20 says:

Where there is no gossip, strife ceases.

Church fellowships seldom fall apart because someone shot the preacher or stole the silverware but backbiting and gossiping have destroyed many fellowships down through the ages.

James affirms that there is but one lawgiver and one judge and we should not attempt to put ourselves in the place of God.

Matthew Chapter 7 Verse 1 says:
Judge not that you be not judged.

Paul makes the statement in Romans Chapter 14 Verse 4:
Who are you to judge someone else's servant? His own master will decide if he stands or falls.

When Peter asked Jesus how many times he should forgive his brother (Matthew Chapter 18 Verse 21) and would seven times be enough, Jesus replied 'No, seventy times seven' or in other words, there is no upper limit to how many times you forgive someone.

The problem comes when someone does or says something that so repulses you that you cannot remain silent about it, because you see it as something which the church cannot condone, like sexual abuse.

Where the leadership is not involved in this offence I believe that you should approach a member of the leadership team with your concerns and give them the opportunity to take action but if you are not satisfied that the matter has been properly dealt with then as a last resort, you have to go to the authorities about your concerns.

Thousands of vulnerable people around the world have been permanently damaged because ordinary God-fearing people did not speak out about the sexual abuse that they knew was going on. **This must never be allowed to happen again.**

13. Come now (and pay attention) all of you who say: Today or tomorrow we will go into this city and we will stay there for a year and trade and make a profit.

14. You do not know what will happen to you tomorrow. For you are a vapour (a mist), appearing for a little while and then you have completely disappeared (vanished).

15. Instead you should be saying: If it is the Lord's will we will be alive and we will be doing this and that.

16. But as it is you brag about your boastful language; all such boastings are evil.

Perhaps James had the parable of the foolish farmer (Luke Chapter 12 Verses 16 to 20) in mind when he wrote those verses:

Jesus told them a parable saying: The land of a certain rich man produced plentifully and he reasoned with himself saying: What shall I do, because I have nowhere to store my crops?

So he said: I will do this, I will pull down my existing barns and build larger ones: and I will gather my wheat and other crops into them and I will say to my soul: Soul, you have many goods stored up for many years; take it easy, eat, drink and be happy.

But God said to him: Foolish man, this very night your soul will be demanded from you; then who will the things you have prepared belong to?

This story is not saying that it is wrong to be successful in business, be it farming, manufacture or anything else; it is asking the question 'Where do your priorities lie?'

Are you so busy serving the needs of your business that you have cut God out of your life?

What part does 'the Lord's will for your life' play in your everyday thinking?

As James points out in Verse 14 our time on this earth is like a cloud of vapour that is here for a moment and then it is gone and since we know that we cannot take our earthly possessions to heaven with us, why do we put such great store in accumulating them and then storing them.

In the parable of the sower (Luke Chapter 8 Verses 1 to 15) Jesus likens the seed which fell among thorns to those who hear the word but become chocked by the *cares and riches and pleasures of life*, so that they fail to reach maturity and produce a harvest.

Each of us needs to take stock from time to time as to whether we have lost our first love like the church at Ephesus (Revelation Chapter 2 Verse 4) and if we have, to pray fervently as to how we can get it back, because Jesus warned us in Matthew Chapter 16 Verse 26:

For what will it benefit a man, if he should gain the whole world, but loses his soul?

We have already discussed being boastful so I will not go over this again but I will quote the apostle Paul (Galatians Chapter 6 Verse 14) who said:

God forbid that I should boast except in the cross of our Lord Jesus Christ.

17. Therefore (I say) to the person who knows the good he ought to do and fails to do it, such a failure is a sin.

When James wrote this warning to Christians I wonder if he had in mind what Jesus said when he preached on how he will judge the nations and what he will to say to those who had not fed the hungry or given drink to the thirsty or hospitality to the stranger or clothed the naked or visited those who were sick or in prison. Matthew Chapter 25 Verses 31 to 46 tells us that he said:

Truthfully I say to you, because you did not give assistance to one of these poor, needy, underprivileged people, you did not give assistance to me.

We cannot turn on our television sets or look at our portable devices without seeing graphic pictures and hearing harrowing details of wars, insurrections, floods, famines, landslips, earthquakes, tsunamis etc. etc. the list seems endless. Most of these incidents happen hundreds, if not thousands of miles from where we live and to peoples we have never met and whose native language we do not understand and whose culture is very different from our own.

Surely James was not suggesting that since we could, in theory, do something to help these millions of desperate people that we are committing a sin if we don't?

I do not believe that is what he was suggesting in Verse 17 and the reason I say this is based on the story in John Chapter 5 Verses 1 to 15 which tells of Jesus visiting the pool of Bethesda in Jerusalem which was situated by the Sheep Gate.

Verse 3 tells us that there was a great multitude of sick people there as well as the blind, paralyzed and lame who were waiting for the waters to be troubled so that they could be first into them in order to be made well again.

Verses 5 to 9 tells how Jesus picked out just one man and healed him alone and then left the pool leaving all the others exactly the same as he found them (from an infirmities point of view).

The same Spirit that was in Jesus is in us and just as Jesus was drawn to that one man, so the Holy Spirit draws us to that person or cause that he wants us to minister to and it is when we deny/ignore the promptings of the Holy Spirit that we are in error and are guilty of sin.

On a practical point, if I had spent my days helping old ladies cross the street, I would have lost my job and me and my family would soon have become homeless and destitute which would have obviously been wrong, but if I had not helped that particular old lady that the Holy Spirit was prompting me to help, then I would have been sinning.

Sometime in the late nineteen seventies or early eighties there was a report in the local paper of a lady hitch-hiker who had threatened a male motorist who had kindly given her a lift that if he didn't take her to where she wanted to go and give her some money then she would go to the police and accuse him of assaulting her.

My wife and I discussed this case and agreed that I would not in the future pick up hitchhikers if I was alone in the car as I often passed them on my way to work.

For some time after coming to this decision I happily drove past hitch-hikers leaving them to their own devices but one day, just I was driving past a person, I felt the Holy Spirit tell me to go back and give him a lift. I drove on for a while struggling with this instruction but eventually turned the car round, picked the person up and dropped him off close to the building I was working in. In thinking about it, I have never been prompted to do that again and have not picked up a hitch-hiker since then.

What each one of us does in response to Verse 17 is between us and the Holy Spirit but we can support worthy causes with our cash, we can support missionary/aid workers which our church/fellowship sponsors and of course we can pray for people and organisations which are out there on the front line helping those in need.

DISCUSSION SUBJECTS FOR CHAPTER FOUR

1. Why can't people get on with each other?

2. Why don't we ask Jesus for things?

3. How do we stay in the world without becoming worldly?

4. How would you explain the concept of *'Submit yourselves therefore, to God'* to a new Christian?

5. Why do we like to gossip and how can we prevent it from damaging our fellowship?

6. What are the good and bad points from using the phrase *'If it is the Lord's will' in our prayers?*

7. How do you know when the Holy Spirit has prompted you to do something?

Chapter Seven
COMMENTARY ON THE BOOK OF JAMES

Chapter Five

1. Come now (and pay attention) you rich people, weep and cry aloud over the hardships which are coming upon you.

After various comments about the rich in Chapters 1 and 2 James has devoted the first six verses of Chapter 5 to warn of the danger of earthly riches and how they can have a corrupting and deadly influence on our lives.

In the second verse of his letter (Chapter 1 Verse 2) he addresses the readers of the letter as 'My brothers' and in the second to last verse of his letter (Chapter 5 Verse 19) he closes the letter with the term 'My brothers' and at different points in the letter he refers to the readers as 'brothers'. I conclude from this that the letter was meant to be read by 'brother' Christians in the different fellowships of the early church and most probably Jewish Christians as Chapter 1 Verse 1 talks of the 'twelve tribes in the dispersion'.

James would appear to be echoing the warning that Jesus gave in Luke Chapter 6 Verse 24 when he said:
But watch out, you who are rich, for you have already received your reward.

The implication seems to be that these are the good times for rich people and things can only get worse in the future, as described in the story of Lazarus and the rich man in Luke Chapter 16 Verses 19 to 31:
Now a certain man was rich and used to put on a purple robe and fine linen and was merry and lived well every day.
And a certain poor man, Lazarus by name, was placed at his gate and was covered with sores.
And he desired to be fed with the things which fell from the rich man's table; but even the dogs, coming to him, licked his sores.
And it came to pass that the poor man died and was carried away by the angels into the bosom of Abraham and the rich man also died and was buried.
But in Hades where he is in torment, he looks up and sees Abraham from afar and Lazarus in his bosom.
And he called to him and said: Father Abraham, have pity on me and send Lazarus that he might dip the tip of his finger in water and may cool my tongue, because I am suffering in this flame.
But Abraham said: Child, remember that during your lifetime you received all those good things but Lazarus

likewise received the bad; but now here, he is comforted and you are suffering.

And besides all this, a great chasm has been firmly fixed between us and you, so that anyone who wishes to pass from here to you, cannot and neither can anyone cross over from there to us.

And he said: I ask you therefore, father, that you might send him to my father's house;

For I have five brothers; so that he might witness to them, in case they also come to this place of torment.

But Abraham says: They have Moses and the prophets, let them hear them.

But he said: No, father Abraham, but if someone from the dead should go to them, they will repent.

But he said to him: If they do not hear Moses and the prophets, neither will they be persuaded if someone should rise again from the dead.

But what is so terrible or wrong about being rich, you might ask?

James sets out the answer to that question in the next few verses.

2. Your riches have become corrupted and your garments have become moth-eaten.

3. Your gold and silver have become rusted over (corrupted) and the poison resulting from this corruption will be a testimony against you and it will consume your flesh like fire. You have stored up treasure in these last days.

Corrupt – lacking in integrity, open to bribery and dishonest practices, morally debased, rotten, putrid, spoilt, infected, tainted and made to be different from the original text (as in a manuscript).

In Luke Chapter 12 Verses 32 to 34 Jesus said:
Fear not little flock, because your Father was very pleased to give you the kingdom.
Sell your possessions and give to those in need, make for yourselves purses that will not become old, a treasure in heaven that will not fail you and where no thief can come near, nor a moth corrupt (eat it).
For where your treasure is, there your heart will be also.

The only other reference I could find about something being 'moth- eaten' was in Job Chapter 13 Verse 28 which says:
Man decays like something which is rotten, just like a garment which is moth-eaten.

Paul writes to Timothy in 1 Timothy Chapter 6 Verse 10:
For the love of money is the root of all evil; which some have hankered after and have wandered from the faith and have pierced themselves through with many pains and sorrows.

Money and riches do not bring about a person's downfall in themselves, it is the 'love' of money and the 'pursuit' of riches and allowing them to replace Jesus at the centre of our lives that causes us to fall.

If you spend much of your time worrying about keeping your riches safe or finding ways to increase them or use them to better effect you cannot be concentrating on what Jesus wants you to do.

Of course we have to work and provide for ourselves and our families and save for our old age but Jesus and James and Paul did not spend a reasonable amount of their time talking and writing about the dangers of being rich, if there wasn't a real problem/danger with being rich!

If you are rich you need to ask yourself the question:
Are my riches coming between me and Jesus?
And if the honest answer is 'Yes they are' then the best thing you can do is to get rid of (or reduce) those riches, just as Jesus advised in Luke Chapter 12 Verse 33:

Sell your possessions and give to those in need, make for yourselves purses that will not become old, a treasure in heaven that will not fail you and where no thief can come near, nor a moth corrupt.

4. Behold, the wages of the workmen who have reaped your lands which you have kept back (and not paid to them), cry out and the cries of those who have been reaping have entered the ears of (been heard by) the Lord of Hosts.

James really does like to tackle the controversial issues of the age head on. Since the time he wrote this letter to the first half of the 20th Century workers in most Western countries were not paid a fair wage and that is probably still true in many third world countries today.

To our shame and horror we discovered towards the end of 2016 that slavery is still operating, albeit on a small scale, in the UK and in many parts of Europe.

We read in the press and hear reports on television that international companies are aware that goods are being made in third world countries by children under the age of ten who are paid just a few pence each day.

The moral dilemma facing each one of us when we go shopping is huge and many find it daunting.

In 1 Corinthians Chapter 9 Verses 1 to 18 Paul argues that he and Barnabas have the right to receive a financial reward for preaching the gospel (Verse 14). In Verse 9 he quotes from Deuteronomy Chapter 25 Verse 4 which says:

You shall not muzzle an ox while it is treading out the grain (working).

And Jesus stated in Luke Chapter 10 Verse 7 when sending out the seventy two disciples:

Remain in the same house, eating and drinking everything with them, *for the workman is worthy of his pay.* Do not move from house to house.

As Christian employers we must be seen to be acting fairly towards those who work for us, whether close by, or at arm's length. Employing an outside contractor (or supplier) to do work for us (or provide goods or services) at a price that would not allow them to pay a fair wage to their employees does not let us off the hook!

If that means that our business is no longer competitive then we need to get down on our knees and start asking God for a solution because breaking his law for business/economic reasons is no more acceptable to him than breaking it out of greed and malice.

In 1 Corinthians Chapter 10 Verses 23 to 33 Paul talks about eating food which has been sacrificed to idols and how that affects our consciences. While this is not the same as buying goods made by slaves or underpaid workers, it does, I believe, give us a guide as to how we should face this dilemma.

In Verse 25 he says:
You are free to eat whatever is sold in the meat market without asking questions because of your conscience.
In Verse 27 he advises that if someone asks you to dinner and puts food before you, that you should eat it with a clear conscience.

His attitude changes in Verse 28, however, where he tells us not to eat food sacrificed to idols where we have been specifically told that it has been offered to an idol, in case our action gives offence to someone else.

From this advice we can deduce that if we go shopping for a certain item and we see something that meets our requirements in our price range then we can buy it with a clear conscience without asking lots of questions about it.

If we actually know or think that a certain item was made unethically by slave or child or underpaid workers or has been acquired through criminal activities, then we should refrain from purchasing that item for the sake of our own conscience and the consciences of anybody else who might be affected by our purchase.

5. You have lived in luxury on the earth and have lived riotously (without restraint, running wild) you nourished your own hearts as in a day of slaughter.

The book of Proverbs contains many warnings about what happens to someone who runs wild and lives riotously and Jesus spoke of this in the parable of the Prodigal Son (Luke Chapter 15 Verses 11 to 32) when he said in verse 13:
And after a few days, having got all his things together, the younger son departed for a far country and there wasted his property, with riotous living.

The son did not enjoy his riotous lifestyle for very long and only found true peace and happiness again when he returned to be with his father and apologised for the way he had squandered all that the father had given to him.

How we live our lives directly affects those around us and as Jesus pointed out in the story of the talents (Matthew Chapter 25 Verses 14 to 30) he expects us to use all of our talents sensibly and for the benefit of his kingdom. They are not there just to give us an easy time because we happen to be more blessed than other people.

The verse concludes by saying:
you nourished your own hearts as in a day of slaughter.

This phrase is not one that I am used to but I believe that it should be taken as a warning. The prophet Zechariah in Chapter 11 of his book in the Old Testament spoke out against those who should have been shepherding the people of Israel and seeing to their needs and spiritual wellbeing but instead were looking after themselves at the expense of those in their care.

He says in Verses 4 and 5:
The Lord my God says, 'Feed the flock for slaughter, whose owners slaughter them and sell them without feeling any guilt and then go on to say, 'Blessed be the Lord for now I am rich' and their shepherds have no pity for them.'

If we accept a leadership position, be it in the church or in business or in the family then we will be accountable to God for how we treat and lead those we are responsible for.

Alternatively *'you nourished your own hearts as in a day of slaughter'* could be a warning of the dangers of living your life as if every day was 'party day' not realising that the day of judgement was just around the corner when you will have to account for your actions or lack of them and for your stewardship of all that God has given to you.

6. You have condemned and murdered innocent people; even though they were not resisting you

We do not know if James had a particular situation in mind when he wrote this verse or whether it was a general observation that the rich and powerful often use their position to commit terrible crimes against the poor and weak such as drumming up false accusations against them and then finding them guilty of crimes they have not committed and punishing them with fines, imprisonment, confiscation of lands and property and even death.

In 1 Kings Chapter 21 we find the story of King Ahab and the vineyard he coveted which belonged to a man named Naboth.

He allowed his evil wife Jezebel to hatch a scheme whereby false witnesses made claims against Naboth which resulted in him being stoned to death and Ahab taking possession of the vineyard.

The prophet Elijah was sent by God to confront Ahab with this evil and to pronounce God's judgement on his family line and in particular on Jezebel, the instigator of the crime.

The story continues in 2 Kings Chapter 9 after Ahab had died and one of his army commanders called Jehu was now king in his place.

Jehu rode into Jezreel where Jezebel was staying and had her thrown out of an upper window by two or three eunuchs. She would have died on impact with the ground, her blood spattering the wall of the house and the roadway. She was trampled underfoot by the horses that were passing that way and what was left of her was eaten by the dogs apart from her skull, feet and hands in fulfilment of Elijah's prophecy against her.

In Numbers Chapter 32 Verse 23 Moses gave this warning to the tribes of Reuben and Gad when he agreed to allow them to live on the other side of the Jordan from the rest of the people on condition that their armed men crossed the Jordan to fight the enemy with the other tribes:

If you do not do what you have said you would do, then take note of this, you would have sinned against the Lord and you can be sure of this, *that your sins will find you out!*

And the same is still true today, if we use our wealth, position or power to ill-treat others then we can expect God's wrath to catch up with us because we are all accountable to him for our actions.

7. Therefore, be longsuffering (patient, enduring insult) brothers, until the coming of the Lord. Behold (consider) the farmer as he waits for the precious crop which the earth produces, watching patiently over it until he gets both the early and late rains.

8. You also must be longsuffering, settle your hearts, because the coming of the Lord is near.

We are told in Genesis Chapter 1 Verse 27 that God created man in his own image, so to understand who we are and what God expects of us, quite obviously, we need to understand who God is and what, exactly, he had to say about himself.

Exodus Chapter 34 Verses 5 and 6 tells us that when God descended in a cloud and spoke to Moses on Mount Sinai he first of all spoke his name and while passing before Moses he proclaimed, 'The Lord, the Lord God, merciful and gracious, *longsuffering* and abundant in goodness and truth.'

If God is a 'longsuffering' God and we are 'made in his image' then it is no wonder that he expects us to be 'longsuffering' too and to take the time and to make the effort to develop that particular fruit of the Spirit so that we can become more like him.

James likens longsuffering to what a farmer has to go through as he waits for the harvest. He has prepared the land, sown the seed, watched the rains come and go and seen the crop slowly grow and ripen and finally, just at the right time he can harvest the crop and store it safely in his barn.

The process is the same today as it was two thousand years ago and in some parts of the world the same methods and tools as used back then are still in use today.

From a Christian perspective, the big difference between now and then is that back then the church were expecting Jesus to return 'any time soon' whereas nowadays, generally speaking, we do not feel the same urgency and many of us are not patiently waiting for the imminent return of Jesus, but are just getting on with our lives believing that it will happen sometime, but probably not in our lifetime.

The three questions we have to ask ourselves, therefore, are:

1. Would I be acting differently if I truly believed that Jesus would be coming back next week?
2. Would the church be acting differently if it truly believed that Jesus would be coming back next week?

3. What would we be doing differently?

9. Do not murmur against (complain about, disparage) one another brothers, for fear that you will be judged; for behold, the judge is standing at the door.

In Chapter 4 Verses 11 and 12 we looked at the dangers of 'backbiting' and 'gossiping' and 'judging others' and how it can tear a fellowship apart and here in Verse 9 James mentions another problem found in Christian fellowships and that is complaining about or disparaging other members of the fellowship and in particular, those in leadership.

For some reason most of us are always ready to complain about others (what they might have said and done that we disagree with), but never think to encourage or congratulate someone when they have done something we do agree with or have benefitted from.

In 1 Timothy Chapter 5 Paul gives advice on how we should behave towards other members of our fellowship.
Verse 1: Do not rebuke an older man but reason with him as if he was your father and treat men younger than yourself as if they were younger brothers.
Verse 2: Treat older women as you would your mother and younger women as you would a sister, with pure thoughts and intentions.
Verse 17: Honour the elders who work for and have charge of your fellowship, especially those who teach and preach.

19. Do not entertain an accusation against an elder unless it is supported by two or three witnesses.

20. Rebuke publicly those who are guilty of sin so that the rest may be fearful of doing something similar.

It is unclear as to whether James is still referring to elders or the whole fellowship in Verse 20, but I am sure it would only apply to serious wrongdoings like immorality.

Revelation Chapter 3 Verse 20 says:
Behold, I stand at the door and knock. If anyone hears my voice and opens the door I will come into his house and I will dine with him and he will dine with me.

John Chapter 5 Verse 22 quotes Jesus as saying:
The Father judges no-one but has committed all judgement to the Son.
And Verse 30 states: My judgement is just.
And Chapter 8 Verse 16 says: My judgement is true.

Jesus will come and he will judge the earth and separate the sheep from the goats (Matthew Chapter 25 Verse 32) as he clearly warned us.

10. As an example of longsuffering under persecution my brothers, take the prophets who spoke in the name of the Lord.

Luke Chapter 6 Verses 22 and 23 informs us:
Blessed are you when men hate you and ostracise you and pick on you and speak your name as if it is something evil, for the Son of man's sake.

When that day happens, rejoice and leap for joy, (for I tell you,) that your reward in heaven is great: for their fathers did exactly the same things to the prophets.

And Verses 27 to 29 go on to say:
Love your enemies, do good to those who hate you, bless anyone who curses you, pray for anyone who insults you.
To the person who hits you on one cheek, turn the other cheek to him as well and if someone should take your cloak from you do not stop him from taking your coat as well.

Longsuffering (patient endurance) under persecution is not something that any of us would seek, but as we well know, many Christians in the 21st Century are having to bear with this today.

I do not feel qualified to comment on this subject but from the testimonies I have heard and read, the Lord certainly does give good gifts to those who ask him and 'patient endurance' is one of those gifts which he gives to those who are in need of it.

11. Behold, we consider those who have endured, to be blessed. You have heard of the endurance of Job and you know of the final outcome that he received from the Lord, for the Lord is compassionate and merciful.

James is not saying that he considers those who have endured persecution are fortunate, he is saying that they are blessed, which is not the same thing.

I recently heard the testimony of a man who grew up in a war zone where he regularly had to dodge bombs and bullets as he went about his daily life. I was amazed to hear that he was not bitter against God but had a faith and an assurance of his salvation which most of us would have to admire. Despite the terrible things he saw and went through, God had certainly blessed him in some amazing ways.

Whilst most of the readers of this book will not have to endure hardships like that, many will have experienced family problems, business/marriage/health breakdowns, bullying, discrimination, criminal activities aimed at them etc. etc. just as Job did and like him, we may not be very happy about it but we can ask for strength to endure the situation while asking God to step in and give us release/relief from it.

Psalm 103 Verse 8 proclaims:
The Lord is compassionate and gracious; slow to anger and abounding in mercy.

We have a heavenly Father who cares about us and a Saviour who intercedes for us; we should never feel that Jesus is not interested in our situation or in providing a way forward for us.

12. But above everything else my brothers, do not swear; neither by heaven nor by earth, nor by any other oath; but let your 'Yes' be 'yes' and your 'No' be 'no', so that you do not fall under judgement.

James is not talking here about taking an oath such as in a court of law or in marriage ceremony or where you are making a declaration about something which you want to be legally binding on you and perhaps on another person or persons. He is saying that in answer to an ordinary question where a simple 'yes' or 'no' will suffice, there is no need to say anything more.

To give a silly example of where swearing would be inappropriate let us consider a motorist who parked his car on a hill and came back some time later to find that it had rolled down the hill into another car and had caused some damage.

The owner of the other car might well accuse the motorist of being negligent in that he did not apply the handbrake properly before he left the car and the accused might say in reply, 'I swear on my dog's life that I did apply the handbrake', where all he needed to say was, 'You are wrong, I did apply the handbrake'. Bringing 'his dog's life' into the discussion does not add anything to his declaration, especially since his dog had played no part in what had happened.

So often in this type of situation people swear by God or Jesus or the saints or the cross or their parents or their children and at worse could be committing blasphemy and at best are making unnecessary references to things or people they hold dear.

James is repeating here some of Jesus' own words that we find in Matthew Chapter 5 Verses 33 to 37 when he spoke about swearing and in particular Verses 34 and 35 when we are told not to swear by heaven or earth and Verse 37, which says:

But let your communication be 'yes and yes' and 'no and no', for whatever you say more than this is evil.

13. Is anyone among you in trouble (afflicted)? Let him pray. Is anyone cheerful (or merry)? Let him sing a psalm.

Every club and society has benefits which the members can enjoy. I belong to a bowling club which allows me to go along and practice, using the greens, mats and jacks which belong to the club. I am permitted to join in club competitions and to represent the club when we have matches against other clubs.

Being a Christian also has benefits and one of them is that when we pray Jesus intercedes with the Father on our behalf and he is never too busy or otherwise occupied to listen to what we have to say and there is no matter which is too small or too big for us to take to him, but as we discussed in Chapter 4, this does not mean that we always get the answer we want!

In quoting from the old King James Version of the bible, the Psalmist talks about the afflicted in many of the Psalms.

Psalm 9 Verse 12 says:
He forgets not the afflicted.
Psalm 22 Verse 24 says:
He has not abhorred the affliction of the afflicted.
Psalm 82 Verse 3 says:
Do justice to the afflicted and needy.
Psalm 140 Verse 12 says:

The Lord will maintain the cause of the afflicted and maintain justice for the poor.

And finally in Psalm 46 which is all about God's willingness to help and his mighty power, Verse 1 starts off with:

God is our refuge and strength, a very present help in times of trouble.

Is anyone cheerful (or merry)? Let him sing a psalm.

To many of those outside the Christian church we have the reputation of being miserable and never smiling which I am sure puts some people off from coming to church.

In the story of the prodigal son Jesus concluded the story in Luke Chapter 15 Verse 32 with the father turning to the eldest son and saying:

It is right for us to be merry and to rejoice, because your brother was dead and has come to life and was lost and is found.

As Christians, we have so much to rejoice (sing) about and I believe that when we meet together that these should be happy enjoyable occasions for us all, albeit that we will have quiet and more solemn times as well and that when we meet in small groups or are on our own then singing a Christian song or chorus can just lift our spirits and fill us with heavenly joy.

Even today, sixty five years on, I still find myself singing the happy joyful choruses I learnt in Sunday school and they always lift my spirit and make me smile.

For Example that lovely children's song by Anna Bartlett Warner:

Jesus loves me this I know, for the bible tells me so;
Little ones to him belong, I am weak but he is strong.

Yes, Jesus loves me. Yes Jesus loves me.
Yes, Jesus loves me. The bible tells me so.

Not only does singing lift our spirits but it can lift the spirits of other worshippers when we are joyously praising the Lord. I think of my old Sunday School Superintendent Mr. H. Matson singing that wonderful old hymn by S. Baring-Gould, first published in 1524, 'Onward Christian Soldiers' and I can hear him now singing at the top of his voice the last two lines of the chorus:

With the cross of Jesus,
Going on before.

Even if, at the start of the hymn, I did not want to sing myself after hearing Mr. Matson sing the chorus a couple of times, I couldn't help but join in praising the Lord and was always lifted and blessed by singing those inspiring words along with him.

14. Is anyone among you sick? Let him summon the elders of the church and let them pray over him, having anointed him with oil in the name of the Lord.

15. And the prayer of faith will heal the one who is sick and the Lord will raise him and if he has sinned it will be forgiven him.

For me, these are two of the most important verses in the whole bible. There are no 'ifs' or 'maybes' in what James has written here; he states categorically what Christians should do when they are sick and what their expectations should be as a result of taking this course of action.

The act of 'summoning the elders' to our house, or 'going to them at their house' or to our place of worship and submitting to their authority clearly demonstrates our faith and our obedience to the word as well as their faith and obedience and the love which we have for Jesus and for each other.

I mentioned above that being a Christian has certain benefits and James is clearly stating in these verses that being healed of our sicknesses is one of them.

On a practical note, we who are sick take the step of faith, the elders anoint us with oil and pray the prayer and God moves in the way he thinks best and not always quite as we expect him to.

The following three examples, which have happened to me and my wife, demonstrate how God can move in answer to the prayer of faith:

About five years ago my wife was seriously ill with gastritis and although the problem was eventually diagnosed and treated by the medical staff of our local hospital her stomach was never quite the same again. About a year ago the problem seemed to be getting worse again so my wife went forward at the end of a morning service for prayer and was duly anointed with oil and the elders of our church started to pray for her. She was suddenly bent double by a searing pain (that she said was identical to the worst of the pains she had suffered with the gastritis) but the elders continued to pray for her and as quickly as the pain had come it went away again and to this day, she has not had the same pain or level of discomfort again.

In 2001 on a trip to Australia I suffered a severe bout of asthma. Over the next few weeks it seemed that every time I went to church that the pastor felt led to invite anyone suffering with asthma to come forward for prayer. Each time the invitation was made I went forward for prayer and each time after the prayer I felt worse than I had before I went forward. It got to the stage when I was willing the pastor not to give the invitation but he always did and I just seemed to get worse and worse. Eventually, things got so bad that my wife took me to the local hospital where I was put on oxygen and given steroids and a nebuliser to use. I used that nebuliser for the next three months and even bought one to take back to England with me. As it turned out I never needed the nebuliser when I got back to England and have not used it in the sixteen years since then and although I am still asthmatic, I have never been as bad since, as I was in 2001.

Sometime in the early nineteen eighties I was working with a lovely Christian man who was an elder of a church not far from Portsmouth in England. On one particular weekend my wife and I were invited to his house for Sunday lunch and to his fellowship meeting beforehand. During the meeting we shared communion in small groups and after the bread and the wine had been taken my friend asked if anyone needed prayer. I had a really bad neck-ache at the time so my friend (and I think his wife) prayed for healing for my neck. As they finished praying for my neck my wife exclaimed that the headache which she had silently been enduring all morning had suddenly gone but my neck ache was no different. The bible tells us that when we marry 'the two shall become one' so God used my neck ache to heal my wife's bad headache because she would have been too shy back then, in strange surroundings, to have asked for prayer. I always joke that I had a 'pain in the neck' and God healed my wife, proving that God has a sense of humour.

> James ends Verse 15 with the sentence:
> *and if he has sinned it will be forgiven him.*
> which is the pre-cursor to what he says in Verse 16.

16. Therefore, confess your sins to one another and pray on behalf of one another so that you might be healed. The fervent prayer of a righteous man is extremely effective.

For those of us not brought up in an environment where we are used to 'confessing our sins' to another person, this verse can present us with quite a challenge.

When James wrote this verse recording devices had not been invented and the thought of confessing something today which the whole world could be watching or listening to tomorrow does leave us in a bit of a quandary and there is no point in being naïve about things like this.

I have myself been in a meeting where the leader was wearing a microphone which he forgot to switch off when praying for someone at the end of the meeting. Fortunately he realised his mistake and removed the microphone before there was any embarrassment.

I should like to point out that when James says *'confess your sins to one another'* he is not saying that we should give intimate details of those things in our lives that we are seeking God's forgiveness for. God knows what is on our minds and why we are asking for forgiveness, the person praying for us does not need to know all that.

I have often prayed for people who needed forgiveness regarding something they have said or done or need help in stopping a particular problem or addiction where I have had no idea whatsoever of what the problem was about but having asked God for 'wisdom', 'knowledge' and 'discernment' before starting my prayer, I have prayed with conviction and certainty about their problem and have seen them set free from their sin.

It is interesting that James links the confessing of our sins to being healed and Jesus also touched on this link to some physical ailments as shown in the story in Luke Chapter 5 Verses 18 to 26 where Jesus healed a paralysed man but before he actually healed the man he said to him in Verse 20:

Man, your sins have been forgiven.

There is certainly an implication here that un-forgiven sin in a person's life can act as a block to their receiving healing from God, but we should not conclude that every time we pray for healing and it does not happen that it is down to un-forgiven sin in that person's life. God alone knows the answer to things like that.

I love the way that James ends verse 16 with the statement:

The fervent prayer of a righteous man is extremely effective.

That is so encouraging for those of us who pray for others, but we do, of course, have to qualify first of all, to being 'a righteous man'. If we should find that our prayers are not being extremely effective then we should check with the Father to make sure that we have not lost or relinquished our 'righteous man' status.

17. Elijah was a man with feelings, just like us and he prayed earnestly that it would not rain and it did not rain on the earth for three years and six months.

18. And he prayed again and the heavens gave rain and the earth brought forth all of its fruits.

The prophet Elijah burst onto the scene in 1 Kings Chapter 17 Verse 1 when he said to King Ahab, 'There shall not be any dew or any rain on the land these years, unless I give the word for it to rain or to deposit dew again.

He then went and hid for three years until God spoke to him again (Chapter 18 Verse 1) and told him to confront Ahab once more and to tell him that the dew and rain would return to the land very soon, which he did in Chapter 18 Verse 41.

I think it would be reasonable to conclude from these two verses that James is telling us that Elijah was a 'righteous man' whose prayers were extremely effective, but James is also telling us that Elijah was a man 'with feelings' just like you and me.

There was nothing special about him, he was just an ordinary faithful man of God who was called for this particular task and ministry and like Elijah, whatever task or ministry we are called to perform, God will answer our prayers in the same way that he answered Elijah's, if we too qualify as righteous men and women doing what he wants us to do.

19. My brothers, if anyone among you wanders from the truth and another one of you turns him back to the truth again;

20. You should know this, that the person who turns a sinner from the error of his way will save his soul from death and will hide a multitude of sins.

In the last two verses of his letter James wants to remind people how essential it is that the truth be preached in all Christian fellowships and that they need to be on their guard to make sure that heresies, lies and half truths do not become established as these will cause the downfall of those who are taken in by them.

Paul mentions the same problems in his various letters and Revelation also talks about some of the early churches losing their way.

Standing up for the true gospel has caused God's people to endure punishment, torture and death down through the ages, but it is because these saints of God have stood their ground that we still have the truth available to us today.

Verses 19 and 20 tell us that it is the responsibility of every believer to be on his guard to protect the truth and to take positive action with those who have been deceived so that they might come back to the truth, if they are born again believers who have strayed and be saved from their sin and from death, if they are unsaved non-believers.

David wrote in Psalm 51 Verse 1 to 6:
Have mercy upon me, O God, because of your great love and kindness: because (the multitude of) your tender mercies are so huge, they blot out all of my wrongdoings.

Thoroughly wash away all my iniquities and cleanse me from my sin.

For I confess my wrongdoings: and my sin is always in front of me.

Against you, you only, have I sinned and done this evil before your eyes. That you might be justified when you speak and be clear when you judge.

Yes, I was shaped for iniquity and my mother conceived me in sin.

I know that you desire truth from within us: and in the hidden parts of my mind you will make me know wisdom.

Because God has a multitude of mercies he is able to forgive a multitude of sins because he desires that we know the truth and that the truth dwells within us.

Jesus said in John Chapter 14 Verse 6:
I am the way and the truth and the life; no one comes to the father, except through me.

And in Luke Chapter 5 Verses 31 and 32 Jesus stated:

Those who are healthy do not need a doctor, but those who are sick. I have not come to call righteous people to repentance but sinners.

No matter what the sin God can forgive it and change a person to become a completely different being and then use them for his purposes.

Consider Moses, David, Simon/Peter, Paul and the many thousands of men and women who became different people after they had given their hearts to the Lord.

The smallest sin separates us from God which is why we all need forgiveness, we all need to be cleansed, saved and born again in order to enjoy life eternal with him.

I urge all of you to read your bible regularly and to get to know what it says for yourself so that you will not be led astray and lose your faith. Don't be afraid to stand up and be counted when things are not right in your fellowship, but do it with love and sincerity, without party spirit and after much prayer and heart searching.

May God bless you all and keep you safe until that great day.

Jude's Blessing

Now to him who is able to keep you from stumbling and to set you, without blemish, before the presence of his glory with rejoicing, to the only true God, our Saviour, who is Jesus Christ our Lord, to him be glory and majesty, dominion and power, both now and for ever.

Amen. Jude verses 24 to 25

DISCUSSION SUBJECTS FOR CHAPTER FIVE

1. Why does James say that being rich is a bad thing?

2. Why does slavery still exist today?

3. What does the farmer have to teach us and why are people today so impatient?

4. Which aspect of persecution worries you most?

5. Discuss *'Is anyone among you in trouble (afflicted)? Let him pray.'* And give examples of where this has worked for you.

6. What is the point of anointing someone with oil?

7. Discuss 'confess your sins to one another'.

8. What may cause someone to wander from the truth?

Chapter Eight

SYNOPSIS OF THE BOOK OF JAMES

	CHAPTER ONE VERSE	CHAPTER TWO VERSE	CHAPTER THREE VERSE	CHAPTER FOUR VERSE	CHAPTER FIVE VERSE
anger management	19, 20,				
asking God	5,6			2,3,	
backbiting				11,12	
be doers	22,23,24				
blasphemy		7,			
blessings	12, 25,				11,
boasting	9,10		5,	16,	
complain/ disparage					9,
conscience					4,
crown	12,				
corruption					2,3,6
deception	16, 26				
desires - wrong	14, 15, 21			1,2,3,5,	
discrimination		1,2,3,4,9			

	CHAPTER ONE VERSE	CHAPTER TWO VERSE	CHAPTER THREE VERSE	CHAPTER FOUR VERSE	CHAPTER FIVE VERSE
draw near to God				8,	
endurance	3,4,				7, 11
ethics					4,6
faith	3, 6	1,5 14 - 26			15,16, 17, 18
faithfulness	12,				
faith - lacking	7,8				
first-fruits	18,				
forgiveness					16,
freedom	25,	12,			
gifts (from God)	17,				
gossip				11,12	
grace of God				6,	
healing					14,15,16
hearing God	19,			15,	
humility	1, 9, 10		13,	6,10,	
hypocrisy			9 to 12	8,	
immorality				4, 5	
in-fighting				1,	
jeolousy/ rivalry			14 to 16	2,	
judgement		13,	1,		9, 12
judging others				11,12,	
law of God	25,	8 to 12		11, 12	
lawbreaker/ sinner		9 to 11			6,15,17,18,19,20
love		8,			
lust	14, 15				
made perfect	4,	22,			
maturity			13,		
mercy		13,	17,		
patience					7,8,10,11

	CHAPTER ONE VERSE	CHAPTER TWO VERSE	CHAPTER THREE VERSE	CHAPTER FOUR VERSE	CHAPTER FIVE VERSE
peacemakers			18,		
persecution					10,11,
poor people		2 to 6			6,
prayer					13,14,1516,17,18
priorities - Christian				13 to 16	
rebuke - devil				7,	
relationships					9,
religion	26,27				
religious	26,27				
repentance				9,	19, 20
respect		1,2,3,4			
rich (worldly)	10,11	5,6			1 to 6,
rich (in faith)		5,			
riotous living					5,
self control - tongue	26,		2 to 12		
servant	1,				
sin	15 21,	11,		17,	15,16
slave	1,				
submission			17,	7,	
suffering	2,				
swearing/ oaths					12,
temptations	13,14,				
titles	1,				
trials	2, 3, 12				
truth					19, 20
warning (leaders)					5,
warning (teachers)			1,2		
wisdom	5,		13 to17		

	CHAPTER ONE VERSE	**CHAPTER TWO VERSE**	**CHAPTER THREE VERSE**	**CHAPTER FOUR VERSE**	**CHAPTER FIVE VERSE**
works (Christian)					
word of truth		14 to 26	13,		
worship/ singing	18,				
					13,

Chapter Nine

PRAYERS YOU MAY FIND USEFUL

Opening Prayers

O Lord, help us to be open to all that you want to say to us today and help us to understand what true compassion (repentance, grace, mercy etc.) is all about.
Amen.

Lord Jesus, give us ears to hear and eyes to see and the intellect to understand all that you want to say to us today.
Amen

Body, mind and soul we give,
To serve the Lord is our desire.
His word to soak into our hearts
Our spirits lit by heavenly fire.
Lord Jesus, please speak clearly to us today.
Amen

God of peace, God of love, creator of the earth,
Each one of us is known by name
And loved by you from birth.
Your love and peace are freely given
Your bounty we enjoy;
Speak to our hearts and minds today
That our lives may bring you joy.
Amen
From the Methodist Sunday Service –
(Revised by Lucidus Smith)

O Lord, our heavenly Father, almighty and everlasting God, who has safely brought us to this day; watch over us and protect us with your mighty power and keep us from committing any sin today and guard us from all forms of danger; but help us to live our lives in accordance with your will and to do that which is right in your sight;

Through Jesus Christ our Lord.
Amen

Psalm 95 Verses 1 to 7A
(Revised by Lucidus Smith)

O come let us sing to the Lord; let us make a joyful noise to the rock of our salvation.

Let us come into his presence with thanksgiving and joyfully sing songs of praise to him.

For the Lord is the great God and a great King above all gods.

He holds the deep places of the earth in his hand; the strength of the hills is also his.

The sea is his and he made it and his hands shaped the dry land.

Come let us worship and bow down; let us kneel before the Lord our maker.

For he is our God and we are the people he cares for and the sheep that he tends.

Amen

Lord of heaven and earth, we praise your Holy name.

Thank you for your love for us and for the forgiveness of our sins, which you achieved by your death on the cross.

We ask that you will be present among us today and that you will empower us through your Holy Spirit and speak to us through your word.

May our praises be pleasing in your sight and may we be the richer for having spent this time with you.

Jesus, you are our Saviour and our friend and we love you and desire to please you. Amen.

God of creation, thank you for allowing us to come into your presence today. As we read your word and praise your name, help us to be attentive to all that you wish to say to us.

With you Father God, nothing is impossible; so fill us with a sense of your wonder and majesty and might, that our faith may be strengthened and our belief in You and your Son Jesus Christ and your Holy Spirit may be multiplied many times over, so that we may be as effective here on earth as you intended us to be. Amen

Opening Prayer for a Mixed Group of People for a Secular Activity

God of the countryside, God of the town,
God of my good days and God when I'm down.
God when we're working and when we're at play
Bless those here tonight Lord and those who're away.
Be with us while dancing (playing/swimming etc)
and share in our glee,
God of eternity, whose love sets us free. Amen

CLOSING PRAYERS – BIBLICAL BLESSINGS

Aaron's Blessing
The Lord bless you and keep you,
The Lord make his face to shine upon you and be gracious to you.
The Lord look favourably upon you and give you peace.
Amen. Numbers 6 verses 24 to 26

Paul's Blessing to the Corinthians
May the grace of the Lord Jesus Christ and the love of God and the fellowship of the Holy Spirit, be with you all.
Amen. 2 Corinthians 13 verse 14

Blessing to the Hebrews
Now may the God of peace, who led up out of the dead, our Lord Jesus, the great shepherd of the sheep, through the blood of the everlasting covenant; make you perfect in every good thing, to enable you to do his will, working in us that which is pleasing in his sight, through Jesus Christ, to whom be glory for ever and ever.
Amen. Hebrews 13 verses 20 to 21

Jude's Blessing

Now to him who is able to keep you from stumbling and to set you, without blemish, before the presence of his glory with rejoicing, to the only true God, our Saviour, who is Jesus Christ our Lord, to him be glory and majesty, dominion and power, both now and for ever.

Amen. Jude verses 24 to 25

CLOSING PRAYERS – OTHER SOURCES

Thank you Jesus, for this time of fellowship with you and with your people.

We ask that you will be with each one of us, as we go our different ways and that you will watch over us and protect and guide us through the coming week.

Give us opportunity to witness to others and the courage to serve you wherever we may be and whatever circumstances we find ourselves in.

May we reflect your love and goodness, to everyone that we meet.

Amen.

Anonymous – but before 1558
God be in my head, And in my understanding.
God be in my eyes, And in my looking.
God be in my mouth, And in my speaking.
God be in my heart, And in my thinking.
God be at my end, And in my departing.
Amen.

Traditional

May the peace of God, which passes all understanding, keep your hearts and minds in the knowledge and love of God and of his son Jesus Christ our Lord;

And may the blessing of God almighty, the Father, the Son and the Holy Spirit, be among you and remain with you always.

Amen

Almighty and most merciful God, thank you for loving us and for sending your Son, Jesus Christ to be our Saviour and friend.

May your Holy Spirit be upon us and go with us and guide us, as we go our separate ways and keep us safe until we meet again.

To you be glory and power and majesty, both now and forever.

Amen

Foundling hospital hymn 1809

Praise the God of our salvation; hosts on high, his power proclaim;

Heaven and earth and all creation, laud and magnify his name.

May God go with you and keep you safe in his Son, our Lord and Saviour, Jesus Christ.

Amen

Lord Jesus, thank you for all that you have done for us and for your courage and for the example that you set us during your time here on earth.

Speak to each one of us in the coming days and show us how we can give ourselves to you and how we can put your will, before our own and love you in the way you deserve.
Amen

Thank you Lord Jesus for this time spent together with you.
Be with us now as we each go our separate ways,
And guide us and protect us and strengthen us, in our daily walk with you.
Amen

Thomas Ken 1637 - 1711
    Praise God from whom all blessings flow;
    Praise him all creatures here below;
    Praise him above you heavenly host;
    Praise Father, Son and Holy Ghost.
    Amen.

Benediction
    May the grace of our Lord Jesus Christ and the love of God and the communion of the Holy Spirit be with you all now and forever. Amen

CHILSDREN'S PRAYERS

Bedtime Prayer - Young Children
    Thank you Jesus
    For the day that's done;
    I have had a lot of fun.
    Food for my tummy
    Shoes for my feet

And bless all the little ones
Who live down my street.
Amen.
(Can be sung to the tune of Baa Baa Black Sheep)

Bedtime Prayer for Older Children
Keep me safe throughout the night,
Let angels guard my bed.
Refresh my body while I sleep
And sweet dreams fill my head.
When I awake tomorrow morn,
Equip me for the day,
And bless the ones who care for me
And help me on my way.
Thank you Jesus - Amen

Children's Grace – Informal A
Thank you for the sky so blue,
For sheep that baa and cows that moo;
For farmers working in the mud,
Lord Jesus, bless this lovely grub.
Amen.

Children's Grace – Informal B
Thank you for the sea so blue
For ships and crabs and fishes too
For mighty waves and stones that crunch
Lord Jesus, bless this lovely lunch.
Amen.

SPECIAL OCCASIONN PRAYERS

LORD'S PRAYER
From the Methodist Sunday Service – 1846

Our Father, who art in heaven, hallowed be thy name; thy kingdom come, thy will be done, on earth as it is in heaven.

Give us this day our daily bread and forgive us our trespasses, as we forgive those who trespass against us.

And lead us not into temptation; but deliver us from evil:

For thine (yours) is the kingdom, the power and the glory;

forever and ever.

Amen

PRAYER TO RECEIVE JESUS AS SAVIOUR AND LORD

Jesus, I want you to be Lord of my life.

I am sorry for all the wrong things that I have said and thought and done, please forgive me and set me free from past mistakes.

I believe that you died on the cross for me and are able to take away all my sins and leave me completely clean.

Come into my heart Lord Jesus, right now and be my Saviour and my friend.

I invite you to take control of my life and to make me into the person you want me to be.

Give me strength for each day and help me to love and serve you, as you deserve.

Amen

RECEIVING THE HOLY SPIRIT

Prayer for an individual believer on their own to be baptized with the Holy Spirit and to be filled with power and with all spiritual gifts – Joe Ewen – Leader of River Churches Scotland.

Father God, thank you for your great love for me and for sending your son, my Lord and Saviour, Jesus Christ, to die for me on the cross, so that through his precious blood, I am forgiven and cleansed of all my sins.

Lord Jesus, I renounce anything in my past that affects me and I ask you to forgive me and cleanse me, and thank you that the past is forgiven and I am free. The devil has no power over me, no place in me and no unsettled claim against me.

Lord Jesus, I ask you to baptise me now in the Holy Spirit and to fill me with Your power so that I may praise and honour you all my days and let me be fully equipped with all spiritual gifts, so that I may serve you faithfully here on earth.

Amen

Prayer for a leader to pray so that others may be baptized with the Holy Spirit and be filled with power and with all spiritual gifts - Joe Ewen – Leader of River Churches Scotland.

Father God, we thank you for your great love for us and for sending your son, our Lord and Saviour, Jesus Christ, to die for us on the cross, so that through his precious blood, we are forgiven and cleansed of all our sins.

I pray Lord Jesus, that if there is anyone present, who has anything affecting them from their past, I take authority with them now and renounce every effect in Jesus' name. The devil has no power over us, no place in us and no unsettled claim against us.

And now, Lord Jesus, please baptize us with the Holy Spirit and fill us with Your power so that we may praise and honour you all our days and let each one of us be fully equipped with all spiritual gifts, so that we may serve you faithfully here on earth. Amen

THE SELKIRK GRACE - Ancient Scottish Grace
Some hae meat and canna eat,
and some wad eat that want it,
but we hae meat and we can eat,
and sae the Lord be thankit.

HEALING
Adult - praying for a sick child-
Dear Lord Jesus, friend of little children, I come to you today, to ask you to make
CHILD'S NAME better.
Because you know everything about us, you know exactly what has made him/her sick and you know exactly what to do to make him/her well, so I am asking you to heal CHILD'S NAME of all illness and side effects, so that he/she can be made fully well and fit and be able to live life to the full.
Amen

A leader praying for a sick Christian after anointing the person with oil.
Wilf Riedy – Pastor - Lighthouse Church Mandurah WA

PERSON'S NAME - by your confession of faith in the Lord Jesus Christ and the healing power of the Blood of Jesus through the stripes he bore on the cross of Calvary for our sicknesses and infirmities – we declare a healing to your body and command this pain and sickness/stiffness to leave and further command your body to line up with the word of God that proclaims you should have life and life more abundantly.

Now receive your healing in Jesus' name and give thanks to the Lord for it.

Amen

A PRAYER FOR THE BEREAVED – Allan Harrison

Loving God, You are the father of all mercies and the giver of all comfort.

As we remember the family of PERSON'S NAME please give them the assurance of Your constant loving care, that they may have courage and strength for the days ahead.

Father, help them in time to work through their sad loss and grant to them comfort and strength as they now face the future without PERSON'S NAME. Surround them with Your great love and goodness at this time.

Remind them all of the good times together with HER/HIM and may their memories remain strong and precious and full!

In the lonely times – sustain them, strengthen them, renew them and draw them close to each other – and to You.

Father - as they look to You - may they all come to know the strength and peace of Your love and goodness. Amen.

THE APOSTLES CREED

I believe in God, the Father Almighty, Maker of heaven and earth and in Jesus Christ, his only Son our Lord: who was conceived by the Holy Ghost; born of the Virgin Mary; suffered under Pontius Pilate; was crucified, died and buried: he descended into hell; the third day he rose again from the dead; he ascended into heaven and sits at the right hand of God the Father Almighty; from there he will come to judge the living and the dead.

I believe in the Holy Ghost, the holy catholic church, the communion of the saints, the forgiveness of sins; the resurrection of the body and the life everlasting. Amen

Chapter Ten

A SHORT STUDY ON THE TEN COMMANDMENTS

Opening Prayer
Lord of heaven and earth, creator God, we know that these are the commandments which you gave to Moses and the children of Israel, written on tablets of stone.

We understand Father, that these are non-negotiable, for they are your law given to us.

Speak to each one of us today and help us to understand and accept them and to live our lives accordingly.

Amen

Bible Passage - Exodus Chapter 20 verses 1 to 17
And God spoke all these words saying:
I am the Lord your God, who has brought you out of the land of Egypt, out of the house of bondage.

You shall have no other gods before me.

You shall not make for yourself any idol or any likeness of anything that is in heaven above, or that is on the earth below, or that is in the waters of the earth:

You shall not bow down (pay homage) to them or serve them: for I, the Lord your God, am a jealous God, allowing the sins of the fathers to affect the children down to the third and fourth generation of those that hate me;

And showing mercy to thousands of those that love me and keep my commandments.

You shall not use the name of the Lord your God carelessly or in a blasphemous manner; for the Lord will not hold anyone blameless that misuses his name.

Remember to keep the Sabbath day holy.

You have six days in which to work and transact your business:

But the seventh day is the Sabbath of the Lord your God: on that day you shall not do any work, not you, nor your son or your daughter, nor your male and female servants, nor your cattle, nor the stranger that is within your household:

For in six days the Lord made heaven and earth and the sea and all that they contain and rested on the seventh day and the Lord blessed the Sabbath day and made it holy.

Honour your father and your mother: that your days may be long in the land which the Lord your God is giving you

You shall not kill.

You shall not commit adultery.

You shall not steal.

You shall not give false testimony against your neighbour (perjury).

You shall not covet (strongly desire) your neighbour's house, you shall not covet your neighbour's wife, nor his male and female servants, nor his ox, nor his ass, nor any other thing that is your neighbour's.

Introductory Notes

God's right to set the laws that we live by.
Genesis 1 verse 1
In the beginning, God created the heaven and the earth.

Proverbs Chapter 8 Verse 23 – Wisdom Speaks.
I was appointed from the beginning, before the world began, to last for all eternity.

John Chapter 1 Verses 1 and 2 - The Word became Flesh.
In the beginning, was the Word, and the Word was with God and the Word was God. The same was with God in the beginning.

Hebrews Chapter 1 Verse 10.
And you Lord, at the beginning, founded the earth; and the heavens are the works of your hands.
God created the heavens and the earth and all that they contain.

I, personally, believe the account of creation as laid out in Genesis, but if you choose to believe something else, it does not, in my opinion, change the fact that the creator of all that we know and call the heavens and the earth is Almighty God.

I believe the Lord Jesus was instrumental in that creation process and I believe that Wisdom was right there at the beginning. That is why his laws are so wise and good for us.

Jesus did not come to change or remove any of the Old Testament law, that is why in Luke Chapter 16 Verse 17 – Jesus said:

But it is easier for the heavens and the earth to pass away, than the smallest punctuation mark of the law to cease to exist.

In Matthew Chapter 22 Verses 35 to 40, is the description of Jesus being questioned about the law.

35. Then one of them who was a lawyer, tempting him asked:

36. Teacher, which is the greatest commandment of the law?

37. And he said to him: You shall love the Lord your God with all your heart and with all your soul and with all your understanding.

38. This is the first and greatest commandment.

39. And the second is like it: You shall love your neighbour as yourself.

40. On these two commandments hang all the law and what the prophets have prophesised.

Jesus expected his hearers to know the Law and what all the prophets had said and to interpret them in line with 'Loving God and your Neighbour'. To fully understand the magnitude and meaning of the first and second commandment, as above, we must have an understanding of the other commandments.

The apostle Paul confirms this to us in 2 Timothy Chapter 3 Verses 16 and 17 – where he says:
All scripture is God breathed (inspired) and can be profitably used for teaching, for reproof, for correction, for instruction in righteousness, in order that the man of God may be perfected for every good work, having been properly trained and equipped.

The Father desires that you are properly trained and equipped, so that you can be ready for every good work.

We were on our way to church a few days after Christmas some years ago when we saw a young lad riding a brand new bike, which we guessed he had been given for Christmas. He was enjoying himself and the pavement was quite wide and he seemed to know what he was doing.

As he approached us we noticed that there was something hanging from the handlebars and as he got nearer we realised it was a crash helmet. Whoever had bought the bike, had also bought a brand new crash helmet for the boy to wear when he was out riding it. The boy had chosen to ride the bike without putting the helmet on, which meant he was exposing himself to unnecessary risk and injury.

Likewise, many people are killed or seriously injured in road accidents every year, because they are not wearing the seat belts which are fitted to the car.

Christians can get hurt and can hurt others, because they are not properly trained and equipped for every good work.

When we became Christians, each one of us was given a unique opportunity to serve God and to do – Good Works = we each had a gift from God, just like the boy had a new bike.

Along with the 'new bike', we also have a crash helmet, it is called the bible.

Do you regularly wear your helmet – or does it normally just hang from the handlebars. Do you read your bible, or does it just sit on a shelf somewhere, looking pretty?

Studying the scriptures should not be an option in your mind, it should be an essential part of your Christian life, for without it, you cannot be properly trained and equipped for every good work and you cannot know when someone is not speaking the truth to you about the things of God.

THE TEN COMMANDMENTS

Exodus Chapter 20
And God spoke all these words saying:
I am the Lord your God, who has brought you out of the land of Egypt, out of the house of bondage.

In these first two verses God is telling the Children of Israel exactly who it is that is speaking to them –

I have not been to Egypt or been a slave, so I changed the first verse so it relates to me rather than the Israelites.

I am the Lord your God, who watched over you during those difficult teenage years, who rescued you out of that motorcycle accident on the Embankment in London when you were 18 and who has guided you through all of your wanderings, ever since.

The First Commandment – Verse 3
You shall have no other gods before me.

The Bible Says:
God created the heavens and the earth.
He also created the forces of nature, wind, waves, fire and seismic pressure.
He also created man and all the animals and everything that grows on the earth.

The forces of nature can change what God created i.e. rock can be worn down to become a pebble or sand.

Man changes what God created to give us timber from trees, metals from ore, plastics from oil, and electronics from lots of other things.
Man continues to discover what God has created, marine life, insects, space etc.

Man is certainly important but God is quite obviously at the top of the pyramid and everything else is below him in importance.
Why would any rational person want to give something or someone pre-eminence over God when he is Number One in importance in the whole universe?

If you are a Christian and God is not Number One in your life, then you have got it wrong!

Do you put yourself first?
Do you put your family first?
Do you put your job first?
Do you put your hobbies first?

Is there anything that you would refuse to give up if God requested it?
Do you trust him with everyone and everything that is important to you?

"You shall have NO other god's before me."

This is not a request – they are called the Ten Commandments and not the Ten Suggestions.
As Christians we have promised to love and serve him and this means to obey his commandments.

NO other God's means just that.

Jesus said in Matthew Chapter 10 Verses 37 to 39:
The one who loves father or mother more than me, is not worthy of me and the one who loves son or daughter more than me, is not worthy of me;
And he who does not take up his cross and follow after me, is not worthy of me.
The one who finds his life, will lose it and the one who loses his life for my sake, will find it.

Jesus is telling us how it should be – he will not accept second place in your life.

This is the first commandment and it is the key to understanding and keeping the other nine commandments.

The Second Commandment – Verses 4 to 5A

You shall not make for yourself any idol or any likeness of anything that is in heaven above, or that is on the earth below, or that is in the waters of the earth:

You shall not bow down (pay homage) to them or serve them;

In Western cultures, having an idol that you bow down to, is not something that most Christians will ever be tempted to do. Having an appreciation of paintings, sculpture, cars, motorbikes, boats, planes, jewellery, clothes and the like is not idolatry, but having a driving desire to acquire and own any of these things, just might be.

If you would rather be attending a market, or shopping mall, or a football match or playing golf or just washing the car than meeting with God's people or doing his work, then you have to start asking yourself whether you have set up an idol in your heart.

Similarly, we do not need to own a special bible or picture, or to be in a special place or situation to find God.

God is Spirit and our spirit can commune with him, anywhere, anytime and in any situation.

In the late nineteen seventies my firm gave me the opportunity to attend an Outward Bound Course at Eskdale in the Lake District in the UK.

Although I did not get much notice, as I was filling in for someone who had to pull out at the last minute, I grabbed the chance to go on the course and incidentally, have a two week break from the office.

About a year before this, I had been filled with the Holy Spirit and although I had been a Christian since I was eleven, I was enjoying a new relationship with the Lord and was looking forward to a real 'Mountain Top' experience with God, during my time away.

The course was great fun and very challenging and we were kept busy for most of the time, but eventually one day the opportunity came along and I climbed my 'mountain' to meet with God.

I sat there for a while, waiting for something spectacular to happen and eventually God spoke quietly to me and this is what I believe he said to me,

"You don't need to be alone on top of a high hill in order to speak with me."

This is so true, in fact, two of the most important revelations I have had from God, came on a crowded commuter train, on my way to work and a Christian friend of mine simply puts his coat on and goes for a walk round town in order to meet with God.

You do not need special aids or icons in order to draw close to God and there is always the risk that eventually they may get in your way.

The carved Snake that Moses lifted up to protect the Children of Israel from snake bites (Numbers Chapter 21 Verses 4 to 9), eventually became a problem and had to be destroyed by King Hezekiah (2 Kings Chapter 18 Verses 3 and 4).

The remainder of Exodus Chapter 20 Verse 5 and Verse 6 warn us of the consequences of breaking this commandment-

For I, the Lord your God, am a jealous God, allowing the sins of the fathers to affect the children down to the third and fourth generation of those that hate me;

And showing mercy to thousands of those that love me and keep my commandments.

The way that we behave can have consequences which affect others for good and for bad, as well as ourselves.

The Third Commandment – Verse 7

You shall not use the name of the Lord your God carelessly or in a blasphemous manner; for the Lord will not hold anyone blameless that misuses his name.

Society today seems to think that blasphemy is OK, but that swearing is not. It is seen as smart, in some circles to blaspheme.

The name of God and of his son Jesus Christ is used instead of swearing and as an exclamation of surprise and as an addition to 'yes' and 'no', as well as in a careless and frivolous manner.

This is the devil's way to devalue the name of God and the name of Jesus.

Let us make sure that we personally, do not blaspheme and that in any area where we have influence, that there is no blasphemy.

Matthew Chapter 5 Verse 37 says:
But let your communication be 'yes and yes' and 'no and no', for whatever you say more than this is evil.

Yes and No are two very powerful words in their own right, they do not need any qualification.

This commandment also carries a warning, for it says: The Lord will not hold anyone blameless that misuses his name.

We need to be very careful in how we use the name of God.

The Fourth Commandment – Verses 8 to 11
Remember to keep the Sabbath day holy.
You have six days in which to work and transact your business:
But the seventh day is the Sabbath of the Lord your God: on that day you shall not do any work, not you, nor your son or your daughter, nor your male and female servants, nor your cattle, nor the stranger that is within your household:
For in six days the Lord made heaven and earth and the sea and all that they contain and rested on the seventh day and the Lord blessed the Sabbath day and made it holy.

For those of us who remember life before Sunday was 'just another day', I would like us to consider how the change has affected us, the ordinary people.

We have-
Less time to go to church and even if we are able to go, some of us will be 'on call' and therefore, will not be able to fully take part and enjoy it.
Less time together as a family as either husband or wife or both, might be working for all or part of the day.
Less time to relax and switch off, because even if we get another day off in the week, it is not going to be as tranquil as Sunday and Sunday is certainly not the tranquil day that it was when I was young.

We are under more stress and more pressure to achieve and with mobile phones and computers, we can now take our work home with us and never really have a break from it.

Unfortunately, for many people, there is no longer any choice about this; as it is now an integral part of many job descriptions and not just an option for those who want to earn double time.

In my opinion, the Quality of Life for ordinary families and for working men and women has gone down with Sunday trading.
If God says we should rest on the Sabbath, then we should try our hardest to do just that.

The Fifth Commandment – Verse 12

Honour your father and your mother: that your days may be long in the land which the Lord your God is giving you.

Paul said in Ephesians Chapter 6 Verses 1 to 3:

Children, obey your parents in the Lord; for this is right.

Honour your father and your mother, which is the first commandment with a promise (which we need to take note of):

In order that it may be well with you and that you may live for a long time on the earth.

I believe this promise is true; therefore the converse is also true.

If you do NOT honour your father and mother-

It will NOT go well with you and you will NOT enjoy a long life on the earth.

I was very fortunate in that I had a fantastic mother and father who loved me and cared for me and looked after me and who I loved very much.

But to my shame I have to say that I did not always 'Honour them' as I should have. On several occasions the Lord has woken me in the middle of the night, to remind me of something I said to my mother during my teenage years, which was not honouring. My mother is dead now, so I cannot apologise to her, but I can confess my wrong-doing to God and ask his forgiveness for what I said to her.

For those who did not have loving parents and who have had bad experiences or maybe are still having bad experiences, you need to ask Jesus to help you deal with this. Similarly, it may be your 'In laws' that give you a problem and once again you must ask Jesus to help you and show you the way forward.

Jesus promised never to leave us or forsake us (Hebrews Chapter 13 Verse 5) and that includes helping us to deal with these sorts of issues.

We need to be very honest with ourselves, as a lot is at stake if we get this one wrong.

If you have a problem in this respect get someone to pray with you about it.

The Sixth Commandment – Verse 13
You shall not kill.
OR You shall not commit murder.

The first crime against man – Cain murdered Abel (Genesis Chapter 4 Verses 1 to 8)

We are also told that Moses murdered an Egyptian, (Exodus Chapter 2 Verses 11 to 15).

David arranged for the death of Uriah the Hittite, (2 Samuel Chapter 11).

Jezebel had Naboth murdered over a vineyard (1 Kings Chapter 21 Verses 1 to 16).

The Jewish leaders had Jesus crucified on a cross like a common criminal (Luke Chapters 22 and 23)

What causes a person to commit murder?

Anger – jealousy – resentment – pride – conceit – hatred – revenge etc. etc.

If we cannot control our emotions, they can lead us into serious trouble and cause severe problems and misery for others.

If these emotions are a problem for you, then you need to get help quickly, for there is no place for them in the heart of a Christian man or woman.

In Paul's letter to the Galatians - Chapter 5 Verses 22 and 23 he says:

But the fruit of the spirit is love, joy, peace, patience, kindness, goodness, faithfulness, gentleness, self-control; against such (fruit) as these, there is no law.

Although 'self-control' is listed last of the nine fruits, for most new Christians it is the fruit we need to learn about first of all. We must be able to control ourselves in order for us to be open to the word of God and the work of the Holy Spirit.

The Seventh Commandment – Verse 14
You shall not commit adultery.

Jesus widened this commandment in Matthew Chapter 5 Verses 27 and 28 when he said:

You have heard that it was said: You shall not commit adultery.

But I am telling you that everyone who looks at a woman with a view to desire her, has already committed adultery with her in his heart.

As we go about our daily life, we are looking at people all the time and there is nothing wrong with that. Jesus was clearly saying that if we look at someone lustfully then in the eyes of God this is unacceptable behaviour.

What Jesus was saying was not a suggestion BUT a Commandment and in today's permissive society we should not expect others to think about this matter in the same way that we Christians do.

We must, therefore, be strong willed and determined to resist temptation whatever the cost.

Remember - Just because you do not make the initial approach, does not make it OK. to sin.

It takes Two to Tango – you can always say NO and simply walk away.

If you have wrongful desires then it might mean that you have to change jobs or move house or leave a club or society, or take a different route to the shops. If you have this problem then get someone you trust to pray for you, so that you do not give way to temptation and fall into sin.

Similarly, if you are being bothered by the unwanted attentions of someone, you need to start praying straight away, that God will intervene and put an end to it and that the Holy Spirit will guide you as to what actions you should take.

You should be aware that first impressions can set the seal on a relationship.
If you speak, act or dress in a flirtatious way, then that is how you will be thought of in the future.

A word of warning to job applicants:
If you come across as flirtatious at an interview for a job, word will soon get around and you will never be free of that reputation.

The Eighth Commandment – Verse 15
You shall not steal.

Let your example in your own household be exemplary.
Every time you steal, you are denying God's ability to provide for you.

In Luke Chapter 12 Verses 6 and 7 Jesus said:
Are not five sparrows sold for two copper coins? But not one of them is forgotten before God.
But even the hairs of your head have all been numbered. Do not be afraid, you are valued more than many sparrows.

God knows about each sparrow and we are much more valuable than a sparrow.

Our heavenly Father knows what we need, even before we ask him.

When it comes to stealing, it is very easy to compare ourselves with the world, rather than with what God's word commands, particularly in the work place.

Buy your own pencils, pens, notebooks, screws, nails and do not 'borrow them' from work.

Do not make OR receive, personal phone calls during work hours, or play computer games.

Do not take time off sick, when you are well enough to go to work – Monday Morning Fever!!

Do not extend your rest breaks.

If you are an employer – then treat your employees fairly and honestly and pay them for what they do in accordance with their contract.

Make sure they are properly trained, equipped and protected for the job that they do.

Stealing is not just putting a brick through a shop window and stealing what is there, it is acquiring anything that you do not have a legal right to.

It is also keeping hold of something which you should be paying out to others, like bus or train fares, or fees or taxes, or our tithes to God.

In Malachi Chapter 3 Verses 8 and 9 God accuses the people of robbing him:

Will a man rob God? Yet you have robbed me. But you say: How have we robbed you?

In tithes and offerings. You have been cursed: for you have robbed me, yes, even this whole nation has robbed me.

In Luke Chapter 20 is the story of a man asking Jesus if they should pay taxes to Caesar? In his reply Jesus says this to them:

So render (submit or give) the things of Caesar, to Caesar and the things of God, to God.

Your family will learn from your example, not from what you might say, so it is very important to make sure that the example in your household is exemplary, both toward man and God.

The Ninth Commandment – Verse 16
You shall not give false testimony against your neighbour (perjury).

To commit Perjury in a court of law – i.e. to accuse someone of something they did not do or say, is a criminal offence.

In 1 Timothy Chapter 5 Verse 13 Paul warns of people who are busybodies or gossips or go around saying things which they ought not.
He happens to be talking about young widows, but the warning applies to us all.

Slander – is the Spoken word – face to face or over the telephone
Libel – is the written word – letters, articles, emails or texts.
Gossip – is to pass on information, (which may even be accurate,) to someone who does not have a need to know it.

In breaking this commandment, we can ruin someone's reputation, take away their friends, lose them their job or home or send them to prison.

People fear being falsely accused-
In this day and age, most men will not pick up a female hitchhiker for fear of being falsely accused.

Adults tend not to greet or help children they do not know any more.
At one time an adult would take a child's hand (even if the child was not known to them) and see them over a dangerous road, now, that simply would not happen.

We can also cause damage by 'Innuendo' – No smoke without fire!!!

Remember - they even tried to blacken the name of Jesus by calling him a drunkard and a glutton.

Be careful how you speak about others, we will have to answer before God, for every unkind word, every malicious rumour and every false accusation we have made.

The Tenth Commandment – Verse 17
You shall not covet (strongly desire) your neighbour's house, you shall not covet your neighbour's wife, nor his male and female servants, nor his ox, nor his ass, nor any other thing that is your neighbour's.

You shall not strongly desire to possess things, which belong to another person.

Jesus said – Luke Chapter 12 Verse 15:
Beware and be on your guard against all forms of covetousness, for a man's life does not abound, in the things he possesses.

Our 'Western' lifestyle is based on a Marketing approach to life. The aim of Marketing is to make us desire all sorts of products we do not have i.e. to make us covet.

Whether it be a new house, sofa, car, clothes, jewellery, holiday, fitness, caravan, lifestyle and so on- we are encouraged to covet all of these things.

One of the major environmental problems we have today is that we are running out of places to dump our rubbish. We are in a throwaway society, where it really is cheaper to make new rather than repair what is old.

When the mini-car was first offered for sale, fifty years ago, it was roughly a working man's wage for a year. It is probably now that same man's wage for about four months.

My DVD player broke down the other year, just out of warranty, and I took it in to have it repaired. It was going to cost me about £65 minimum to repair it, so I bought a brand new one for £55.

When I was young, I had two shirts for school, one for best, two shirts for play and one for work; about six shirts in all.

A quick count of my wardrobe revealed I currently have about 32 shirts in various colours and materials. These include business shirts, casual shirts, work shirts, sports shirts and T shirts.

Can I really convince myself that I do not have a problem with COVETING!!

To be honest – most people have a problem with Coveting and I think we all need to pray for help in keeping this 10th Commandment.

In Conclusion

Moses says in Deuteronomy Chapter 5 Verse 22 after God had finished speaking:

These are the words which the Lord spoke, with a mighty voice, to the whole assembly of the people at the mountain; out of the middle of the fiery cloud and thick darkness and he added nothing else and he wrote them on two stone tablets which he gave to me.

The voice of God delivered these commandments, in person, to the whole Jewish nation. He meant them to be learnt, understood and lived by.

As Christians – we too are children of Abraham and we need to receive them afresh today as coming directly from God himself.

Read them at home, meditate on them and allow them to speak to you.

Let them form the basis of your walk with God and ensure that you are properly trained and equipped, so that you can be ready for every good work.

Closing Prayer

Lord God, please give us a better understanding of your commandments and a willingness to receive your instruction and to change into the people you would want us to be.

Help us in particular to deal with covetousness in this modern age and to live holy and upright lives.

Amen

DISCUSSION SUBJECTS FOR THE TEN COMMANDMENTS

1. What idols do people worship in the 21st Century?

2. 2.   How should you deal with blasphemy in the workplace?

3. How should your church/fellowship accommodate people who have to work on the Sabbath?

4. How do you honour someone who has treated you badly?

5. What effect does TV and films have on our understanding of murder?

6. Why is sexual immorality such a problem today?

7. What form of stealing is considered normal?

8. Discuss the implications of perjury.

9. What are today's temptations that would make us break the 10th commandment?

THE END

Lightning Source UK Ltd.
Milton Keynes UK
UKOW03f0336250417
299826UK00001B/26/P